POTTERS FIELD

BY GAVIN MITCHELL

The dedication should be obvious, but, spoilers.

1.

'Look, there's a seal.'

'He has a fish.'

'One more fish than we've got.'

'Must be a harbour seal.'

'Well we're in a harbour.'

'So it's not just a clever name.'

Dean and Noel sat in a boat with fishing rods held desultorily in loose hands, lines dangling in the water. Beside them were a jar of writhing maggots and an entirely empty bucket, intended for their catch.

'Looks like it's coming on to rain,'

'I guess that concludes this afternoon's entertainment.'

The two rowed back to the renter and returned the boat and all their gear. Above them, the skies grew rapidly cloudier.

'So that was fishing,' said Dean as they made their way back into the city.

'Some of our finite supply of cash gone on an enterprise which did not bring the expected, or any, reward,' observed Noel, whose idea fishing hadn't been.

'Remind me why we came to a port city again?'

'There was... the unpleasantness.'

'Ah yes. That.'

Passing a particular building Dean stopped dead. 'Mind if we go in here?' he asked. His companion acquiesced. Noel found himself in a church in which his friend was already studiously gazing at the decoration. He was used to Dean generally wanting to go in churches, though as he observed that the painting at the head of the building was of a haloed woman in expensive garb holding an ornate jar he concluded that the visit would be longer than usual. Noel decided to sit and get some rest while his companion walked around, and as he had expected he heard a tinkle of coin from the location of the head painting (one more coin that they no longer had, thought Noel, though he did not really begrudge his friend the indulgence) and watched his companion light a candle.

The two would perhaps have lingered a while longer for their various purposes, particularly given the worsening weather outside, but this was cut short by the emergence of the church official wanting to lock up, and they had to return to the ungentle night.

It was now raining steadily, the weather was cold, and the two men were dressed for neither condition. Among large swathes of graffiti proclaiming UNIVERSAL SUFFRAGE and NO TAXATION WITHOUT REPRESENTATION and DEMOCRACY NOW a professionally lettered sign stood out in stark contrast. It stated *The Chemical Wedding – Free Event* and was apparently up some stairs in a run down terrace of buildings and happening now.

'How about having a look in here?' Dean offered.

'It will at least be dry,'

The two made their way upstairs and found themselves sitting in a long gallery with wooden seats laid out in rows, a silent audience watching two figures up front. Dean and Noel positioned themselves in the back row of seats and resolved to sit quietly – if nothing else it was indeed dry, and warm into the bargain.

It transpired that the performance was a stylized unarmed battle between the man and woman interspersed with gestures of affection such as caresses, temporary clinches, kissing of hands and the like. Dean found the martial techniques and the choreography to be competent, if not staggering – he had seen far more dangerous stunts from tumblers and acrobats. However Dean started to find himself increasingly aggravated by the quite audible mutterings of the person sat next to him, which was apparently a commentary on the moves being carried out. *White ape offers fruit – breaking the lotus – sweep the 1000 enemy* and the like. However not only did the names seem to bear no resemblance to what was being displayed they had no resemblance to anything Dean was familiar with, and he fancied himself no slouch in hand to hand combat.

He dug his companion in the ribs. 'If you will keep passing comment at least make it accurate!' he hissed.

Yet the other man continued. He appeared to be in his late twenties with an unflattering combination of slicked down centre parting and bearded chin without moustache, but however wore an apparently quite expensive if unostentatious tunic. *Needle at sea bottom – Buddha pounds pestle into mortar* and so on. It was irritating and Dean (already damp, cold and tired) was only just starting to get warm, and hoping he could craftily get some shut-eye sat here at the back without anyone noticing, which the muttering companion was preventing. He also had a host of other worries of which the performance was not sufficient distraction and the muttered narration kept dragging him back to.

The final straw was when he was dropping off to a blessed sleep but an indrawn hissing breath from next to him brought him back to unwelcome troubling wakefulness. His frustration boiled over. 'I'll show you white ape offers fruit!' he snarled, the volume shockingly loud in the otherwise silent gallery. He surged up out of his chair and dragged the mutterer bodily backwards over his own chair to the floor, following him down. The young man's arms came up in some sort of defence but Dean forcibly crossed both his opponent's arms over his chest.

Someone coughed. Dean looked up to find a number of sturdy looking event officials standing over him. 'I'm going to have to ask you gentlemen to leave,' said one, and stuck his thumbs in his belt. There was no option but to comply.

Outside it had at least stopped raining. 'Thanks for getting us kicked out of there, dickwad!' said Dean in a rage, aiming a kick at the mutterer's shins in fury.

The other man minced away. 'It's not me who decided to start an altercation,' he said primly in a plummy accent.

'I'll give you altercation-'

'Gentlemen,' interrupted Noel in soothing tones. 'There's no need for this unpleasantness.'

The two belligerents backed away from each other, looking sheepish. Dean was well aware of Noel's ability to defuse nasty situations, but had to admit that even if you were expecting it it worked, even on him.

'I'm very sorry for my friend's aggressiveness,' continued Noel. Dean was about to pipe up to argue, but the other man spoke over him. 'We are cold and tired and have travelled far today, and my companion's nerves are sadly frayed. I'm sure we can exchange apologies and smooth things over a few drinks.'

Even though he had seen this a hundred times before Dean was still amazed that it worked. He also had no doubt that their new friend would be paying for those drinks, and probably also food. There was little other option – himself and Noel could never have afforded it.

Even factoring Noel's powers of pacification into account the young man's enthusiasm about taking them for drinks was surprisingly great. He led them to a hostelry which for Dean and Noel was quite upper class, but for himself was probably slumming if anything. He agreed enthusiastically to meeting any tab (the waiter looking over Dean and Noel's worn and travel stained garb with considerable doubt and disdain) and seemed almost childishly grateful to have the opportunity to make new friends with anyone – even someone who had attacked him and got him kicked out of an event not minutes ago. Dean and Noel could only wonder if he had many, or any, real friends in his everyday life.

Drinks did indeed turn into food, and miracle of miracles, the paying in advance of the night's accommodation at the hostelry for Dean and Noel. There was even an agreement in advance for Aurelius (the new companion's name as it turned out; who was, as the two out-of-towners had guessed, a scion of one of the patrician families, the old-money upper class of this town) to meet Dean and Noel tomorrow morning for unspecified activities before he made his way back to his habitual home, presumably a mansion in the better region of the city where the two rougher characters would not at all be welcome.

'Should we really go ahead with meeting him tomorrow or should we make a sharp exit?' said Dean as they were turning in.

'Ach, let's indulge the lad. It's obviously just some excitement for him and he has given us a lot.'

'You're right, let's exploit this meal ticket for as long as possible.'

'Let's go easy on him though, eh? I know you shouldn't give a sucker an even break, but let's not outright shaft people who don't deserve it.'

'Fair comment.'

The next morning Dean and Noel luxuriated in steaming baths and then a sumptuous breakfast before reluctantly leaving the hostelry (who seemed entirely glad to see the back of them) and meeting Aurelius at the appointed hour. Their new friend greeted them with childish enthusiasm. However, the three of them were then somewhat at a loss as to what exactly they should do with their time.

'What's all this DEMOCRACY NOW business then?' said Dean randomly, catching sight of some more of the graffiti.

'Oh, that's a populist movement,' said Aurelius airily, turning and gazing at the words painted on the wall, or possibly a crude depiction of sexual intercourse graffitied underneath them. 'Saying everyone should have a say in the governance of the city and other bizarre ideas. Mostly harmless, except for a few radicals that want to bring down the patricians, which really isn't on.'

'UNIVERSAL SUFFRAGE?'

'Basically that everyone should have a vote, including women and people who don't own property. Madness if you ask me, they wouldn't have the education or intelligence to know what they would be voting for.'

'Quite,' muttered Noel.

'So what do people do for this democracy and suffrage then?'

'Oh, collect signatures on petitions, take donations...'

'*Donations????*'

CHING!

And so before very long Dean and Noel (having 'borrowed' some coins from Aurelius) had rented a trestle table and folding chairs from a party goods warehouse and purchased some paper and writing implements from a stationer. They set the lot up in front of some of the thickest deposits of democracy graffiti and sat down behind the table to await developments, with the legends PETITION and DONATIONS displayed prominently. Before long signatures were going down on the paper and coins were clinking into the conveniently placed pouches.

'I say, it's awfully good of you chaps to start collecting for the democracy cause so soon after arriving in the city,' gushed Aurelius.

'Isn't it,' muttered Dean, watching some coins trickle into one of the emptiest of their pouches.

Most passers by ignored the table and its display completely. Some glanced over but did not otherwise slow their transit. A significant fraction however halted and wrote their signature, and another significant fraction made a donation. Unfortunately however, a few wanted to have a discussion. These ranged from quite reasonable individuals who could be fobbed off by agreements or nods and smiles, to those who wanted to go into deranged rants and others who grew progressively more unhinged. A few times Dean and Noel had to drop their hands to the hilts of their weapons and gaze coldly at the unwelcome individuals to get them to go away. This did not strike them as unusual; it was a frequent tactic of theirs from their previous lives outside the city. Sometimes it degenerated into violence, more often it didn't.

It did not occur to them, however, that they had not seen a single other person carrying weapons, or that their own garb obviously marked them out as being from outside the city, particularly Noel's belted plaid great kilt. Potters Field was a cosmopolitan city as might be expected from a port, with foreigners not being at all remarkable, but most outsiders stuck close to the docks or conducted their own business before departing, rather than heading far into the inner city and engaging in questionable financial solicitation.

Some time into the exercise as Aurelius watched the pouches grow increasingly filled. 'I say,' he said, 'you *are* going to give this money to the democracy movement?'

'Of course,' said Noel smoothly.

'Just not all of it,' said Dean *sotto voce*.

'Or much,' muttered Noel.

'Huh?' said Aurelius.

But suddenly a palpable silence descended on the table and its surroundings. Dean and Noel noticed that there were no longer any citizenry approaching the table and the area around it had distinctly emptied. An uneasy feeling descended upon them. They looked up to see six rough-looking men holding axes and crowbars, accompanying a seventh, a middle-aged, refined looking gentlemen wearing a toga, that notoriously impractical garment, the first they had seen.

'Oh, crap,' muttered Dean. Aurelius's face acquired a look like he'd eaten a dead baby. His mouth opened comically like a letterbox. Noel merely raised his eyebrows.

'Please allow me to introduce myself,' said the gentlemen. 'I am Lord Cromwell, plebeian aedile, and these men are vigiles, with duties including law enforcement. I'm here investigating reports of an unauthorised charity engaged in unsanctioned solicitations and potentially breaching the peace and suborning the public good. And you, gentlemen, having been caught red handed, are under arrest.'

Dean shrugged. 'It's a fair cop,' he said.

2.

While Aurelius was clearly good for nothing at this point and looked as though he might be about to cry, Dean and Noel were both independently considering their chances of fighting their way out (and knew that their opposite number was doing so also). They weren't great. While their own weapons were superior to those carried by the vigiles (which were technically meant for firefighting) axes and crowbars were quite lethal enough on their own and Dean and Noel would each be outnumbered by two or three times. The vigiles looked like hard men who had led harsh lives who could not simply be overpowered or intimidated easily, but would be more inclined to strike down an opponent while they were engaged with a colleague. The aedile was standing well behind his troops and couldn't just be grabbed as a hostage. They were encircled and running was impossible. They were also sitting down which was not a good position from which to launch an attack. Dean had other abilities he could use but it was a bad idea to display them here; and even if they won, a pitched battle with law enforcement would no doubt bring about worse consequences further down the line. Dean and Noel both independently came to the conclusion that it was better to go along quietly; they exchanged a glance and their looks told each other that they had both decided the same.

Aurelius was unarmed but Dean and Noel were stripped of all obvious weapons and several not so obvious. This was not to say that they were both left completely unarmed, but the holdout arms they had managed to retain would have been worse than useless in this situation. There was no attempt to tie or restrain anyone but each of the men was closely flanked and they were marched off, the aedile confiscating the ill-gotten gains and the democracy petitions (Dean wondered bitterly if they might be used as a list of state undesirables further down the line) and marching confidently in front, one hand holding the toga in place (the necessity for this always indicated that the man with the toga was in charge, as he was otherwise incapable of doing anything).

The procession eventually found themselves at what was evidently the aedile's office. Lord Cromwell had the guards usher the three miscreants into a room and then wait outside. The aedile sat down at a desk; the others had no option but to stand before it like naughty schoolchildren.

'Now then,' said Lord Cromwell, leaning forward and steepling his fingers. 'What am I to do with you lawbreakers? I have lots of choices, it seems. You two are obviously out of towners. You carry weapons which is not approved here. Your clothing is uncharacteristic for the city, particularly *that-*' indicating the belted plaid. 'It will probably not surprise you to learn that as outsiders you have no rights at all here. We don't go in for imprisonment in this town, but I could simply have you flogged and escorted to the city gates, or just *beheaded.* I might be reluctant to do this if I suspected you were respected citizens of a foreign power who would take it as a great affront if their beloved sons were mistreated, but somehow I don't think that is the case, is it?

'And as for you, Aurelius, many would consider it shocking that someone in your position belonging to such a noble family would be caught up in something so scandalous. Of course your family protects you and I can't really do anything to you, but what do you think public knowledge of this would do to your house's reputation? Or your future political career? My dear boy, you are in the soup.'

Dean glanced over at Aurelius. The boy was pale and trembling with head downcast, his mouth half open and quivering; he seemed on the verge of wetting himself. 'Pull yourself together man!' he barked.

'Silence!' snapped the aedile. 'I have absolute power over you all from this point forward. I can destroy and ruin you. And yet I am prepared to offer you a way out. You belong to me now. That means

I release you and you can go about your daily lives, but any time I have any shite task going I call for you and you had better come. You do what I want and I don't make this affair public knowledge... or worse. And don't try to leave town or tell anyone else. I'll find out and have you brought back here. Then I'll take one of the other options for your punishments. Capisce?'

Dean cast surreptitious glances at his companions. He was shocked to see a touch of optimism on both their faces. Noel might indeed have reasonably been expected to be beheaded out of hand, while for Aurelius working for an aedile might well be a hand up into political life. He was rather less pleased himself, thinking his choices were to die like a dog or live like a slave. And yet he was committed to go along with Noel.

'Now get out. I'll send for you all later.'

3.

They had left into the presence of the aedile's clerk, who had asked for their domiciles. When Aurelius started to speak the scribe had coldly stated that he knew that patrician family well, which made the boy look even more upset. Subsequently he had turned to Dean and Noel; the younger man, without any other option presenting itself, had blurted out the name of the fairly well-heeled hostelry Aurelius had engaged for them yesterday. The clerk then icily told them to go there and await developments.

Faced with little other option Dean and Noel had complied. On going to the desk they were surprised to find the clerk reacting to them with stammering deference and stating that the aedile was bankrolling their accommodation for the foreseeable future. They had also been promoted into markedly better rooms.

'This is the life, eh?' said Noel as they went to their new and improved accommodation.

'It's what he wants us to do in exchange for it,' muttered Dean.

Even so they decided to run up a very large tab at the aedile's expense in the hotel bar and restaurant, an enterprise at which they succeeded in flying colours and enjoyed a lot.

Next day with thick heads from hangovers worse than usual they awoke to a message that Lord Cromwell wanted to see them. Given the power the aedile wielded in the city it seemed best to comply.

On arrival they were surprised to find Aurelius was not present, there were two chairs put for them in front of the desk, and Cromwell greeted them politely and offered them wine. They accepted it eagerly, hoping hair of the dog would be in effect.

'Sorry about the more coercive aspects of our arrangement,' the aedile began. His manner was much different than the day before, treating them more like equals than misbehaving children. Perhaps the headmaster ritual had been for Aurelius's benefit. 'You will of course be paid. I need some men I can make use of. People who can do things my agents in the city might not.'

'And aren't tied to you and give you plausible deniability,' Noel commented.

'There is also that perhaps. You do also need Aurelius. A patrician can go places in this town no one else can. But I'll assign him to you in due time.'

'So what's so nasty that an aedile needs... out of towners,' said Dean sardonically.

The aedile got up and went to the window, gazing out. The action seemed quite rehearsed.

'People assume that this city is called Potters Field because of someone of that name, or because of actual potters. It is not. How well do you gentlemen know your Gospel?' The aedile looked over his shoulder.

Noel glanced at Dean who gazed blankly off at the wall. Lord Cromwell raised his eyebrows.

'Well, anyway, perhaps you are familiar with the story of Judas Iscariot.'

Cromwell fiddled with the window hangings as he stared out, this also seemed rehearsed. 'Judas betrayed Our Lord Jesus Christ for thirty pieces of silver. Repenting of his act he returned the money to the temple authorities and hanged himself. However, the priests determined that it was blood money, and therefore illegal to be put into their treasury. They decided instead to use it to buy a potter's field – land that was unsuitable for building or agriculture because deep trenches and holes were left after clay had been dug out for use in making ceramics. They subsequently turned the potter's field into a burial ground for strangers, and because it had been bought with blood money it came to be called Aceldama – the place of blood.'

Dean and Noel stared at the aedile's broad back but otherwise made no comment. Cromwell returned to his desk, sat down, clasped his hands and stared at them. 'What do you know of this town?' he asked.

Dean and Noel were nonplussed. They were not sure what they were being asked. People fleeing unpleasantness did not typically consult tourist guidebooks for options.

Seeing their bafflement the aedile elaborated. 'What strikes you from walking around the place, meeting its people, visiting its hostelries. One word is fine if you can't think of anything else.'

Dean and Noel exchanged glances, obviously still puzzled. With no other options Dean spoke. 'Rich?'

The aedile slapped the table top. 'Exactly! This city is indeed rich, certainly the richest city in the region, possibly the richest city in the world. Rich, corrupt, venal and greedy, with its reputation preceding it.'

It was surprising to hear a city official describing his own town as corrupt, as well as the other words. Dean and Noel stared.

'The corruption in this city is legendary. It seems to work in its favour somehow -- the wealth only increases -- but many good people are left broken and destitute, and actions are rarely if ever done on merit. There's been attempts to clean it up but all have failed, with a regularity that some have found surprising. Even electing supposedly incorruptible men to public post is ineffective, it isn't long before they're taking kickbacks and advancing their cronies like all the rest, and acting so greedy that their mothers no longer recognise them. It's said that the bureaucratic system favours corruption or that it's part of the culture and inescapable but it seems to go deeper than that. And organised crime is endemic. It seems to go hand in hand with the government and everyone turns a blind eye. Our last duumvirate was more or less openly backed by pirates.

'I try to keep my business above board, even though the backhanders are far more tempting than I expected them to be. The level of temptation they exerted was surprising, far in excess of the actual value of the money being offered. I came to feel that there was something more to it, that there had to be something else to it, there had to.

'Then I happened along an ancient forgotten legend and it all fell into place.

'This city has its name because it is the final resting place of the thirty pieces of silver given to Judas Iscariot.'

Silence fell. Dean and Noel stared at the aedile. The story was fantastical and it seemed unreal that they would be sat in the office of a sober official wielding considerable power who was telling them this. The Christian priests made out that their stories were true even more so than those of any of the other religions, but even they had to acknowledge that all those events happened over a thousand years ago. It was inconceivable that those thirty pieces of silver could still be in existence somewhere all clustered together after all this time – if they had ever existed at all.

Lord Cromwell cleared his throat. 'It would be a reasonable task to contract you to find these thirty pieces of silver so they could be disposed of, even though most would object to the city losing its apparent golden goose, and I can see from your expressions that you don't believe this story in any case. However the situation has taken on an additional urgency. There has been a marked increase in very nasty crime – ritual murders, desecration of churches and temples and the like. Satanic symbols have been found painted in blood at the crime scenes and there's been evidence of animal sacrifices – and worse. We hear rumours and have gained intelligence that there's been an influx of Satanic cults into the city and they've been winning people over to their side – perhaps the reason is that they've heard of the thirty pieces of silver and want them for this own purposes. Even if the silver is a myth, obviously the crime needs to be dealt with, and it's beyond the talents of the vigiles. Crime here is about money – these crimes are just senseless killing with no profit. It has to stop.

'Needless to say, this is what you gentlemen are tasked with.'

Dean and Noel exchanged glances. 'Plus we're expendable and it's not as though we had any choice anyway.'

'You're not wrong, and that's the spirit. In any case I've said my piece and that'll be all for today. You may as well go back to your hotel and await developments.'

4.

The two hapless operatives found themselves called back early that very evening, before they had had time to restart drinking in the bar at the aedile's expense.

Aurelius was in the aedile's office on this occasion and had been granted a seat for the first time, where he sat slumped and wearing an expression with an odd mixture of unhappy and hopeful. Also present and seated was a young woman with short hair and what seemed a perpetual asymmetrical grin, wearing an outfit leaving her arms and legs bare, which would be very unusual and attract attention in this city and most others. Dean stared, though Noel gave no sign of doing so. There were two empty seats which the two newcomers took without ceremony – and helped themselves to wine.

'Welcome, gentlemen,' said the aedile. 'Aurelius you already know, but I have taken the liberty of adding Ishtar, priestess of Astarte, to your numbers for this mission.'

Noel inclined his head. Dean, still staring, nodded perfunctorily. She raised his eyebrows at his frank regard; the out of towner stared back unrepentant.

'You obviously know about the Democracy Now movement – it's how we met after all.' Aurelius coughed. 'On its own the movement is relatively harmless and has not yet done anything illegal enough to require severe action. We have of course taken the liberty of placing some of our deep cover operatives within the movement to await developments.'

That managed to tear Dean's eyes from the smooth limbs of the priestess and he switched his gaze to the aedile, looking affronted. Cromwell stared back as unabashed as when the out of towner had looked back at the priestess.

'Our operatives had no problems with the movement itself or its legitimate members but they have reported a disturbing frequency of known members of Satanic cults joining. While present these Satanists have been agitating the genuine democracy activists to engage in more extreme acts, including property damage and even attacking people. This has been happening in increasing numbers to the point that it is advisable that special operatives be sent in. You, my friends, are those specials.'

'The Specials. Great,' Dean muttered.

The aedile frowned. 'There is a meeting tonight of one of the pro-democracy factions, a fairly large gathering at St Francis's church hall on the Gideon Hill. I want yourselves to go along to it and join the meeting as interested parties, and see what you can see.'

There was a silence. The four supposed special operatives stared back at Lord Cromwell blankly. He looked irritated and made a flicking motion with his hand. 'Toodles!' he said. There was no option but to leave.

The four made their way to the Gideon Hill on foot. 'So do your duties include all of the functions of a priestess of Astarte?' Dean inquired of Ishtar without preamble.

'They do, but not where *you're* concerned.'

'You walked right into that, my friend,' said Noel, managing to sound sympathetic and avoid a mocking tone. 'Though I myself am curious as to why you would be using a *nom de guerre*.'

She stared back at the older man in surprise. 'What makes you think that?'

'I've seen enough to know that Ishtar is an alternative name for Astarte, so it's unlikely to have been your birth name.'

The priestess looked impressed. 'You're right, of course. Ishtar is a name we are permitted to use when we go on missions such as these. Most people don't realise there's any significance.'

Noel smiled. 'Well, perhaps one day we will have earned enough respect and honour to call you by your true name.'

The girl smiled apparently spontaneously. With most people the comment would have been cringeworthy, but the older man had enough dignity and gravitas to pull it off.

'I've never met a priestess of Astarte,' said Aurelius, still wearing a hopeful yet apprehensive look.

'It's not often I'm privileged to meet a patrician,' replied Ishtar. Again with most people this would have sounded condescending and sarcastic, but she managed to make it sound warm and welcoming. Aurelius blushed and smiled.

It was not long till they reached the church hall, a notice on the door announcing the meeting openly. They were greeted at the door and ushered towards a row of chairs. There were at least a hundred people present with more filing in. Looking around, it was not just the expected poor people, though certainly there were enough of those. There were those whose clothes ran the gamut of social strata, including the well off and extremely rich, even a few patricians.

What there was not, though, was any way to tell if anyone was secretly a Satanist.

Speeches began at the front of the room, though more people came in individually and sat down throughout. The operatives were all united in finding the talks stultifyingly boring. All of them, despite their best efforts, fell asleep at various points during the speeches. This went on for hours. Eventually the talks ended and the speakers, presumably ringleaders, got down from the stage and started having discussions with members of the audience. This did not involve them talking any less.

Dean nudged Noel. 'I don't think we can learn anything here. Let's leave.' They found the other two who happily agreed. The four pushed through what was now quite a considerable crowd and left unannounced.

They made their way back through what was now full night. 'You know, I'm not sure we actually learned anything there,' said Aurelius, managing to sound genuinely surprised.

'Really,' muttered Dean. And then suddenly they noticed a silence.

It was surely no coincidence that this was the darkest street they had come down, virtually entirely unlit. As one the operatives looked up and saw the silhouetted figures of five men blocking their way ahead.

'Good evening,' one of them said, his face in shadow. 'So it seems you four have taken an interest in the Democracy movement. Four people who we wouldn't expect to find associating together. And who we wouldn't expect to take any interest in democracy to begin with. Personally, I find that suspicious.'

All four operatives took involuntary looks behind them. Their exit to the rear was blocked by another five silhouettes.

There was obviously only one way this was going to go.

All four of the special operatives started preparing for battle. Dean started chanting and waving his hands. Most of the attackers stared nonplussed, though one cursed and took a quick step forward. Too late. Blasts of energy lanced from the outsider's hands into the face and throat of the man who had reacted. He screamed, clutched his face, fell and did not rise again. There was general alarm and shouting now amongst the assailants and they rushed the operatives all together. But the others were also ready to fight by now.

Noel drew with practised speed a heavy basket-hilted broadsword with his left hand and a sgian dubh dirk with his right. He immediately moved to engage the largest and most heavily armed enemy. Like him, the attacker was fighting with a sword in one hand and a main-gauche dagger in the other. The weapons clashed, and Noel found his opponent to be both fast and skilled. However, the basket-hilted broadsword was heavier than most swords, and the sgian dubh was unusual. More critically, the opponent fought with his long sword in his right hand and his shorter, lighter dagger in his left, as did most people. Noel fought with the heavy broadsword in his left and the sgian dubh in his right. This was confusing, but his enemy was also skilled. Their battle continued.

Two men wielding daggers headed purposefully towards Aurelius. The patrician was unarmed, and remained so, merely backing away with a look of surprise and his hands raised. His opponents smirked, and one took a lunge. It was thus even more of a shock when Aurelius nimbly sidestepped this, turned into his enemy's side body while gripping the wrist with the dagger and sent him flying into his companion. Both men fell heavily to the cobbles, one dropping his dagger, with Aurelius now having opportunity to smirk. The first to get up bellowed incoherently and rushed the patrician in a rage. Aurelius merely repeated a similar move and sent the man flying head over heels, hitting the cobblestoned road heavily with his head striking with a disturbing crack. Now the second enemy looked at Aurelius with alarm.

More men advanced on the priestess, who again appeared unarmed. Their smirks had a different quality and clearly indicated that they expected the battle to go favourably for them in more than one way. The priestess smiled back, coquettishly. She locked eyes with one assailant, drew a finger down her cleavage, tilted her leg and pursed her lips. The man's eyes glazed over... and he turned and stabbed his colleague fatally through the ribs. 'Why!' shrieked the stricken man as he collapsed. Another enemy looked at the priestess in shock. She smirked and produced a thick rod from inside her costume. The opponent stared in confusion... but Ishtar flicked her wrist and the interior mechanism of the rod shot out with the speed of an asp, telescoping out into a metal baton with a weighted end. She stepped forward without delay and smashed this into the assailant's temple. He collapsed.

Meanwhile Dean had put another of the enemy to sleep; though, seeing him still apparently unarmed, one more man decided to rush the outsider, dagger held out. This availed the assailant naught as with blinding speed, Dean produced a rapier and buckler. The dagger clanged off the small shield and the slim blade pierced through the enemy's throat. Dean withdrew the rapier and his opponent's eyes turned up in death.

Before long all of the attackers had been dealt with with the exception of the big man Noel was duelling and one who Aurelius had face down on the cobblestones in an arm lock, alternating between curses and gasps of pain as the patrician put pressure on the limb. 'Fuck's sake, Aurelius, you're supposed to kill them,' snapped Dean, stepping forward and summarily executing the miscreant. His heart pierced by the rapier, the enemy expired with a groan. 'He would have done the same to you.'

Aurelius stood up sheepishly. Noel and the remaining assailant were battling. Both were clearly superbly skilled fighters and the enemy was a huge, strong man, even bigger than Noel, who was not small. The priestess was looking on entranced at the dance of death, and Dean and Aurelius could only stand and stare with her. Had the attacker been free to engage with the others it was likely that the battle would have gone very differently; observing the assailant's size, strength and skill, each of the operatives independently concluded that they could not have faced him with martial prowess alone, possibly not even with their enhanced abilities. Only Noel tying the man up with swordplay had prevented this.

The enemy seemed to have the upper hand. Probably without the unfamiliarity of facing an opponent who fought with his arms conventionally reversed, and unusual arms at that, the assailant would already have won. Noel showed no sign of fear on his set face, but he was no longer a young man and was breathing heavily. The attacked was younger and had no shortness of breath. He smirked, clearly expecting to win and then face the other three, who he evidently counted no threat.

'Give it up, old man, you've given it your best shot.'

'Not yet,' said Noel through gritted teeth, his breath starting to become ragged, the fatal development for any athlete.

Aurelius started forward, clearly wanting to intervene, but Dean raised a hand. 'Wait,' he said. 'You'll want to see this.'

'Why won't you yield? You must know you've lost,' grated Noel's opponent.

'I do not think so,' answered the kilted man.

'Why not? I'll kill your friends quickly if that helps.'

'Because.'

'Because what?'

'I am not left handed.'

With a quick movement, Noel stepped back and threw both weapons up horizontally. He deftly caught each with the opposite hand... and went for his opponent with redoubled fury. It was obvious to the observers that Noel's skill had increased by another level, by an order of magnitude... and the enemy's had not. His eyes went wide with horror, but he had no time for any more expressions or decisions as the basket-hilted broadsword took him through the ribs.

The last of the assailants fell, and the alley went quiet.

'You are very skilled with the unarmed combat,' said Ishtar, gazing at the patrician with admiration that was possibly only partially feigned. Noel nodded with eyebrows raised. Even Dean looked grudgingly impressed. 'Yeah, where did you learn that?'

Aurelius blushed and smiled, looking embarrassed. 'Well, weapons are frowned on here, even more so for patricians, so I thought I would try this as a hobby. Turns out I was good at it.'

'Keep it up,' said Ishtar and winked at the young man. He stammered something grateful.

A cursory search of the bodies turned up only small change, certainly no evidence that would explain who the attackers were working for or what their agenda was. Ishtar said she would report back to the aedile and the others could return to their homes. They duly complied.

Some time later, Dean and Noel were in the bar of their hotel working on their latest in a succession of drinks, as usual, on Lord Cromwell's tab. A silence had fallen as they stared into space.

'The aedile set us up to get jumped, didn't he?' said Dean.

'Of course he did.'

'You knew?'

'Of course. It was blindingly obvious.'

'I guess it was at that.'

'We turn up in a group looking as outlandish as can be, with none of us the sort who would normally be interested in a meeting like that or would associate together. Even the mercs commented on that. Had we been sensible we would have made some effort to disguise ourselves as tradesmen or labourers or something, then arrived separately and stayed apart. Cromwell never suggested this, and knew it wouldn't occur to us either.'

'So what has he achieved?'

'He's forced the enemy's hand, they're going to know they're down ten bodies, if not how or why. Makes them worry, lets them know we're taking an interest, that it won't be plain sailing.'

'But then they're going to be looking out more for infiltrators.'

'Yes. And while they're going after the obvious expendable ones – us – they don't notice the competent, deep cover operatives.'

'Great,' muttered Dean, draining the rest of his drink and ordering another.

5.

The next summons from the aedile came a few days later, just as Dean and Noel were getting tired of drinking at the aedile's expense and were considering what the rest of the city had to offer. Still they found themselves sat once again in Lord Cromwell's office with the priestess and the patrician – though this time, there was another figure.

'Gentlemen and lady, you've all done excellently,' the aedile began. 'The enemy have sustained a significant loss and they know they are facing determined and powerful opposition. However I feel it is time to introduce a change in tactics. May I introduce another operative, Kunoichi, who will brief you on the next stage in our strategy.

'Another assumed name,' Dean muttered. Noel rolled his eyes.

A woman stood up and went round to the back of Cromwell's chair, where the aedile leaned forward and steepled his fingers, staring at them all. 'I'll get straight to the point.'

By comparison with the priestess, no one would have looked at her twice. In all probability no one would have looked at her twice in any other circumstances either. She was clad in the drab outfit of a fishmonger, which included shapeless clothes and even a hair covering which completely masked any identifying characteristics or body shape. It was not even possible to determine the colour of her eyes. It became rapidly apparent that this was deliberate; her manner and body language seemed designed to avoid attention. It was unlikely she would do such speechifying as followed in her deep cover roles, for such was her obvious purpose.

'Another Democracy Now meeting is taking place later today which we will be attending. However. You need to adopt a fundamental alteration in approach next time you want to infiltrate anything whatsoever. To start with you need working or lower middle class costume. Nothing that will stand out. That especially means no patrician clothing, no priestess uniform, no – whatever that is – (gesturing at the great kilt belted plaid). You are marginally better, but you are still obviously out of town,' she waved at Dean. 'You also need to lose any unconcealable weapons. They are a major red flag here. I have a stockpile of suitable clothing and I will assist in your disguising yourselves.

'You also need to arrive separately and at different times and not clearly know each other when you're there. I would have thought that was obvious, but apparently not.' Dean and Noel raised their eyebrows at one another.

Thus it was that the operatives found themselves kitted out as members of various nondescript professions. Noel was clad as a labourer, the great kilt belted plaid gone – Dean was unable to remember when he'd seen him last without it. The priestess was clad as a middle class housewife – 'I resisted the first offer of prostitute,' she commented drily. Aurelius had been outfitted as a student. Dean had been given the costume of a scribe – 'I *am* coming up in the world,' was his response. The kunoichi merely raised her eyebrows. She herself retained her fishmonger clothing – she had even managed to replicate the smell.

More concerning had been the loss of weapons. Noel had been reduced to his sgian dubh dirk which he had managed to conceal. Dean had deliberately bemoaned the loss of his rapier and buckler and made a great show of hiding a dagger about his person, all the while hoping he had managed to deflect attention away from the *other* concealed weapons he was hoping it was beyond the skills of the kunoichi to notice – though he feared this was unlikely. Aurelius habitually went unarmed in any case. Ishtar had presumably squirreled her extending rod away somewhere. Whatever armament the kunoichi had, she did not reveal it to the other operatives ahead of time.

The plan was then that the team would split up a considerable distance from the venue and approach it at different times and from different angles. This went ahead as agreed. Dean, finding himself on his own, went to the meeting at the agreed time from the agreed direction and found that once again it was a community hall... with the same stultifying speeches. He sat himself down unobtrusively and resisted the urge to look round for his compatriots.

Dean did at least manage to stay awake this time. Once again the speeches were a morass of ideology – while suffocatingly dull, there was also again nothing criminal that could be detected. He hoped that there might be more to be gained in the discussions after the talks.

The speeches did eventually end and people started clearing the seats away (though it wasn't clear if they were associated with the movement or belonged to the venue.) The audience started breaking into groups and talking, though some just left. Dean was debating with himself whether to approach one of the chair stackers, the speech makers or the discussion groups when he heard a deep voice in his ear.

'I don't believe I've seen you around here before.'

Dean turned to his side and found himself staring up at a tall figure with an eyepatch. While he hoped he was still being inconspicuous – and his companions' disguises were obviously working, as he had not yet noticed any of them – this person seemed to be trying to do the opposite. His clothing was so expensive it could only have been afforded by the upper classes or the aristocracy, his hair was styled in long curled ringlets that were clearly artificial, and – unprecedented for this city – he wore a rapier and a dagger, both with jewelled and expensively decorated hilts. And, while previously the venue had been so crowded he had been having to push past people to get anywhere, Dean was now surrounded by a very considerable radius – a bubble that included the newcomer and himself.

Dean had a bad feeling, which only kept increasing.

'Just thought I'd check out one of these rallies,' the out-of-towner mumbled, looking down in consternation, which is what he hoped the reaction of a scribe would also be if confronted by a presumed aristocrat.

'I see. So was there any particular part of the Democracy Now ideology which you found particularly notable?'

Dean's mind raced. If he pleaded total ignorance it would mark him out as an obvious plant, particularly since a scribe would certainly be educated enough to understand what he'd been listening to. The operative thanked his stars he hadn't fallen asleep this time. 'I was quite impressed with the notion of universal enfranchisement, your honour.'

'Really? So do you think that votes for all would be a good thing?'

'Well, it does mean that power would theoretically no longer be in the hands of the richest, those who hold the power anyway. However votes for everyone means that by definition, everyone will have it, and that includes the lowest common denominator; a demographic who are likely to be swayed by demagogues skilled at oratory who will be serving their own agenda, the gutter press, or other such factors. There is also the potential that they could be told how to vote by their employers or landlords or-' Dean stuttered to a halt as he realised he was answering back with far more confidence than a scribe could be expected to show to an aristocrat. He was also staring the man full in the face, the one remaining eye gazing back at him in amusement. Dean lowered his head in consternation.

The tall man smirked. 'An interesting viewpoint, one showing a considerable depth of thinking. I believe I shall have to follow your progress quite closely... *scribe.*' He strode away. Dean stared after him, wondering what kind of can of worms he had just opened.

Later on, it was time for the operatives agreed rendezvous, a quiet park in a different area of town. As Dean approached he noted that their number had now increased to six. Ishtar had with her, gazing at her adoringly, a particularly ill-favoured young man; with missing teeth, hair that looked like it had been cut at random, clothes that looked like he'd been sleeping rough, and a terrible smell that confirmed it.

'Hello again, everyone,' said the priestess with no preamble. 'As you can see I've made a new friend. Loverboy here was inciting the activists to be more violent in their protests – fortunately with no success – but when I approached him, he realised he had better things to do with his time, didn't you, dearest?'

'That's absolutely right, sweetness,' said the oaf adoringly.

'And he told me something very interesting. There's a peaceful march through town for democracy coming up but the Satanists are planning to disrupt it and turn it to violence. Isn't that right my darling?'

'It's true, sugar bunny!'

'So he agreed to come with me. That's most important now, isn't it?'

'Absolutely.'

Dean frowned, wondering at the morality of these tactics. Still, if this guy was inciting violence, he probably deserved what he would no doubt get.

'Good work, Ishtar,' said Noel in genuine praise.

'Yes, impressive,' said the kunoichi, possibly with a sour note.

'So the next stage is to take him to Lord Cromwell for enhanced interrogation,' said the priestess.

'Wait... Cromwell?' said the cretin, his dumb smile fading.

Ishtar gestured, and that was all it took for Aurelius and the kunoichi to grab and lock both the Satanist's arms. 'But... but what will he do to me, darling?'

'Have you tortured till you tell us everything you know about the cultists' operations, I imagine.'

Dean reckoned he could pinpoint the exact moment at which the priestess's spell stopped working. The miscreant screamed, and did not stop screaming again. With some irritation Ishtar produced a gag, which was fashioned as a wooden ball which had had breathing holes drilled through it and which fitted into the mouth and strapped behind the head; Dean had seen enough to know that the purpose of such devices was primarily sexual rather than law enforcement. The Satanist carried on screaming, but at least it was muffled.

'Anyway, why were you talking to the Marquis of Aceldama?' said the kunoichi to Dean in suspicion.

Dean felt his hackles rise. 'He approached me! I didn't know who he was.'

'Why would he be taking an interest in you?'

'I have no idea. I don't think I like your attitude.'

'Look, try not to make this about personalities,' Ishtar interjected, standing between Dean and the kunoichi and addressing the out of towner. 'You have to understand that the Marquis is one of the most powerful people in this city and one of the most shady. Fingers in all kind of nasty pies though nothing can be proven of course. If he's involved in this it's bad news.'

'We have to talk to Cromwell. You'll have to tell him everything that was said,' said the kunoichi, looking at Dean mistrustfully.

'So long as I don't wind up being tortured as well.'

'You should be safe... for now.'

6.

After the debrief it was several days before the aedile called on the team again, presumably long enough for the captive to be exposed to the skills of Cromwell's interrogators. It was certainly long enough for Dean and Noel to finally get tired of the bar and decide to start visiting the city's cultural installations, rapidly finding that there were more museums, galleries, churches and so on than they could visit in the time window. Before they were anywhere near exhausting them all the operatives were summoned.

'We have gained as much information from the Satanist as we could,' explained the aedile. 'Unfortunately he's bottom level, a no hoper wanting revenge on the world but with no great skills to contribute to this goal. He was nowhere near the leadership of the cult and has no idea who they are. His only knowledge about the plan to disrupt the Democracy Now rally comes from a comment he apparently wasn't meant to hear. We need more information otherwise we have no hope of preventing whatever it is they plan to do. The one saving grace is that our friend did know their meeting location. This particular cell have taken over an area of the sewer and managed to avoid notice, or suborned it. You're going to have to go down there and get more intelligence, otherwise this rally could be a massacre... or a takeover.'

The operatives stood silently, looking grim.

'And, Dean. I know we discussed this extensively during the debrief, but has anything come to your mind whatsoever that might explain the interest taken in you by the Marquis?'

The operative scowled. 'Nothing whatsoever.'

'What was your background before you came here?'

'My background is not relevant to anything. I wasn't aware you wanted anything other than a no good street punk to do your dirty work.'

'That is also true. However your background may be of superlative importance in this case.'

'Why?'

No one answered. Dean saw that the kunoichi, the priestess and the aedile were all gazing at him with identical fixed, curious expressions. Noel looked uneasy. Aurelius just looked confused.

'Stop that!' Dean snapped. It had little effect.

Eventually Cromwell shook himself. 'Well, we will have to leave that for now. It is of supreme importance and urgency that you go to this sewer and find out what the Satanists plan for this rally. And don't fuck up.'

The aedile had supplied them with a map and it was not difficult to find the entrance to the sewer, a storm drain leading underneath a hostelry called the Green Dragon. It had been well disguised – the gate looked as rusty and dirty as if it had not been opened in a hundred years – but Dean and the kunoichi found by careful manipulation that some of the bars and metal pieces had been engineered to move, and they eventually gained entry. Inside was an access ladder which also appeared to be almost entirely rust, but which had been repaired and strengthened and then had rust stuck back on. The team descended into the darkness.

They found themselves plunged into waist deep, stinking water, with the only light coming from their own sources. So far this was entirely up to expectations and they had been given extensive directions about how to navigate to the cell's hideout. Still the smell and the disgust factor were precisely as may be imagined, and they winced and squirmed at the occasional human turds or dead rats floating by.

The team made their way along their indicated route. Occasionally the path rose and they were walking on dry land, but all too often they were plunged into the sewage again, deep enough so the kunoichi's feet no longer touched bottom and she had to swim, a fixed wince on her face. Eventually though, they found their first major confirmation point, a door of no particular markings up above the water, which they had been told was the start of the Satanist's territory. It appeared swollen and jammed, but again, Dean and the kunoichi found the trick of its opening. Holding their breath, they went inside.

'What the Hell is that?'

Immediately on entering the room their views were arrested by a giant painting, spreading out over the whole of one door and covering the entirety of the wall it was located in, then spilling onto the adjacent walls and the ceiling. It was a stylised mural depicting a demonic figure. Noel had been the first to speak.

'*Belphegor*,' Dean spat the word with genuine hatred.

'Who is Belphegor?' asked the kunoichi.

'A demon, a lieutenant of Hell and one of its seven princes, and one who stagnates all that which cannot be attributed to itself. Originally a member of the principalities among the angels but now opposes Tiphareth, the sixth Sephiroth of the Qabalah. Can appear as a beautiful naked woman or a monstrous male demon. But he's best known as... the enemy of St Mary Magdalene.'

'Ah,' said Noel.

'But why is he depicted on the *toilet*?' said Aurelius in incredulity.

Dean shrugged. 'He just is.'

'Well, it couldn't be any clearer that we've found what we're looking for,' Ishtar commented.

'It's almost like the Satanists want to announce their presence,' said the kunoichi.

'Maybe if they're this sure of themselves they'll be overconfident and easier to kill!' said Aurelius hopefully. No one answered.

'Right,' muttered Dean after some time. 'So who's going to go to be the first to go through the Belphegor door, then?'

There was no overabundance of eagerness to be the first to go through the Belphegor door. Eventually Noel clicked his tongue in annoyance and stepped forward. The handle turned and the door opened easily, hopefully another sign of overconfidence. Or justified confidence.

The areas of the sewer beyond the threshold did not appear to be in much better repair than those previously. In particular there were still the same extensive areas of flooding, with their attendant turds. The operatives grimaced but otherwise made their way. They were getting closer and closer to the place marked as the central meeting location of the Satanists.

However before reaching it they were abruptly surprised. On opening one door, with nothing to distinguish it from the others, they found the room beyond was lit by lanterns, painfully bright after the gloom. There were also three figures within, initially looking away but immediately whirling to face the intruders. They were a male dressed in heavy armour, marking the first time Dean and Noel had seen anyone armoured since arriving in the city; a female wearing loose dark mottled clothing and several belts of knives and blades; and a figure in robe and hood.

It was the hooded figure that reacted first, lifting up its hands in front of itself and chanting.

'Down!' grated Dean. As one the operatives threw themselves to the floor. Roaring sheets of flame plumed from the figure, gouting over them. None fully escaped being burned, only adrenaline stopping the immediate onslaught of pain.

'Get the caster!' Dean barked, dragging himself painfully to his feet and stumbling toward the robed figure. That opponent, however, started backing away, behind his compatriots. Noel drew his weapons and headed purposefully towards the armoured man, who clashed his weapon against his shield in acknowledgement and stepped forward. Aurelius and the kunoichi ran for the dark-clad female, who drew out a blade in each hand. Dean and Ishtar started circling, trying to reach the robed figure.

The kunoichi proved to be surprisingly and blindingly fast, reaching the other woman before anyone else could get to their chosen opponents. With one hand she flicked open a black fan with metal-reinforced slats with a loud report. The woman's eyes flicked towards the distraction, just on cue for the kunoichi to smash her nose with the heel of her other hand. Regrettably, this gave only a temporary advantage. Blood pouring from her nostrils, the eyes either side of the mashed nose widened with fury. She lunged at the kunoichi with similar speed. Only the kunoichi's own quickness saved her from being lethally stabbed as she jerked back, but she groaned as both daggers scored deeply across her lower ribs on either side.

Meanwhile Noel was attacking the armoured man with furious blows, getting up in his face as much as possible. However it was obvious that the kilted man was doing this to protect his companions and keep this powerful opponent from them, and the eyes behind the helm showed that he was obviously smirking. With his opponent having a shield, full helmet and chainmail Noel could make little impression on the armoured man, and meanwhile Noel's determination to fully occupy the man's attention meant his diligence to his own defence was decreased; before long Noel was bleeding from a dozen wounds. And above all else it was obvious to any observer that Noel was past sixty; in a battle depending on endurance this was not an advantage. The fight continued.

As the robed figure backed away Dean issued some snarls and gestures of his own, and streaks of force launched from his hand aiming at the opponent unerringly. They would have struck had the robed figure not thrown up an invisible barrier in front of itself, against which the darts struck harmlessly. Dean let out a flood of foul language. Ishtar drew herself up, stroked her hands over her torso and started crooning in Babylonian; the hooded figure merely responded with an obscene gesture. That was clearly a no-sell.

The kunoichi had dropped her slatted fan and pulled out two more that were solid iron, weapons known as tessen. These were a match for the other woman's daggers and a rapid chorus of clangs soon filled the chamber as each attacked and parried, searching for an opening. But the kunoichi was bleeding badly from her opened ribs while the busted nose of the enemy was no real hindrance. Meanwhile Aurelius was dodging back and forth at the side of the two armed combatants, trying to get in quick enough to get a wrist or arm lock on the enemy knifer. More often than not he just ended up being slashed, and soon his sleeves were soaked with blood and his arms and hands were cut to ribbons. He had been lucky so far not to lose any fingers.

Noel was now panting raggedly and had taken a deep wound to the thigh that was bleeding heavily, the robed figure had had time to deploy several fire attacks which had left Dean and Ishtar scorched and leaking plasma from areas burned black, and the lips of the kunoichi were turning blue, her face already deathly pale. But for one thing the Satanists would have won. 'Back off!' snarled Aurelius suddenly, and physically shoved the kunoichi back and away. She stared at him in shock. 'Let me take her!'

Aurelius stood before the enemy knifer in his standard martial stance, his face stern. The opponent looked at him with incredulity shading into amusement. 'Bring it!' the patrician snarled.

The woman, now clearly wanting to laugh, stabbed out at him with her dagger. Her overconfidence was to prove fatal. Aurelius brought his hand forward and let the blade impale him completely through the palm up to the hilt. The woman stared at this in shock, her mouth dropping open, and this was all the pause Aurelius needed to lock her wrist with his other hand and break it, then kick her other knife from her grasp. He smashed her chin with an upward elbow strike; she went down.

With the balance now five against two the equilibrium shifted quickly. Turning their backs on the caster Aurelius and the kunoichi could use circling and entering steps to get behind him, at which point he was easily knocked unconscious. Then as one, the four unengaged operatives rammed into the back of the armoured man, who was sent crashing to the floor and held down with their combined weight. The kunoichi applied a garrotte till he fell unconscious with a gurgle.

'Take them alive!' spat the kunoichi, even though half-collapsing with blood loss. 'They must be interrogated.'

'Let me heal our injuries,' Ishtar said, and with accompanying prayers in Babylonian this was duly done, leaving none to doubt the power of Astarte if they had already.

'Well, that was a bit sticky,' said Aurelius, staring at his hand which now looked as though it had never been injured, healed along with everyone else's burns, cuts and contusions.

'The important thing is that *we* survived,' muttered Dean.

'That was an excellent idea you had there,' Noel said, putting his hand on Aurelius's shoulder. 'If you hadn't thought of that, we would all have died. You've saved us all.'

The others all murmured thanks, with varying degrees of sincerity and enthusiasm.

Aurelius blushed, smiled and stammered. 'Oh, it was nothing,'

Dean crowed. 'Oh well that's all right then!'

Noel patted the patrician's shoulder. 'You are being practised upon, my young friend. Pay no attention to my miserable companion. You have been very brave and very resourceful.'

Dean scowled. 'Let's just get out of here. I'm not looking forward to dragging this shower of cunts through the shit.'

7.

The next briefing did not come till several days after the team's exit from the sewer – later than any of them had expected, and almost nearly too late as it turned out. On arrival at Cromwell's office the aedile, always so unflappable and confident before, could be seen to be looking distinctly worried. As well he might.

'Let me start by educating you about the three people you captured,' began Lord Cromwell without preamble. 'The fighter and the assassin were hired muscle only, no ideology or interest in anything the Satanists were doing other than carrying out acts of violence and getting paid. It's almost tempting to let them go without charge. But I'm not gonna.'

The aedile smiled without humour. No one laughed. Cromwell coughed.

'The third was however a genuine black magician, one of those who gravitate to cults such as that so they can hide there-in and gain raw material for their power-seeking blasphemy. No particular commitment to the ideology but well respected by the Satanic commanders, taken into their confidences and consulted for advice on their plans. Strong willed also. It has taken till now to break him, and early on we had to call in a Christian priest to assist from there on. The breaking had to be mental and spiritual as well as physical.'

Dean and Ishtar winced. The kunoichi and Noel looked nauseated. Aurelius just looked confused. 'But why-' started the patrician.

Dean kicked him. 'Not now, idiot,' he hissed.

'What we eventually learned was not good, and had the magician broken a day later it would have been too late. The Satanists plan to disrupt the biggest pro democracy rally yet. To start with they will have agents inciting violence and engaging in random bloodletting on the ground in the rally itself. But these are cannon fodder intended to be caught. They will *also* have operators located on the rooftops armed with crossbows. Their duties are to shoot randomly into the marchers and the crowd so the deaths get blamed on either side and incite more hatred. They intend to orchestrate a bloodbath. It will set the cause of democracy back a thousand years, though that may not even be the intention, compared to the chaos and loss of life. And that rally begins-'

'Tomorrow morning,' said Ishtar, with a look of horror.

'Can you not have the rally called off?' asked Noel.

Cromwell shook his head. 'Impossible. That will be seen by the democracy faction as a clear message that their movement is being suppressed, whatever reason we might give, true or not. This will redouble popular support for them and potentially drive them underground. Right now the movement is entirely visible and entirely peaceful. Perceived aggression will almost certainly make them more secretive and less bloodless.'

'So what's the plan,' grated Dean.

The aedile looked distinctly green. 'I am pulling in my entire force of vigiles from all across the city. We can only hope no fires start or no crimes are committed anywhere else during the duration of the rally. Some groups will be assigned to yourselves and some groups will operate independently. Noel, Ishtar, Aurelius, I want you on the ground marching with the rally or following its progress in the crowds. Dean and Kunoichi, you will each have a squad of vigiles and you will each follow the progress of the march along the rooftops at either side of the road. Kunoichi this should be like tripping from a curb for one of your training, Dean I have no doubt you are familiar with second story work.'

'I'll take that as a compliment,' said Dean drily.

'Each of you must suppress any hostile agents or outbreaks of violence that you find. And God help us all if the city burns down or someone nicks the crown jewels in the interim.'

8.

The pro democracy rally went ahead as planned. The intention was for the suffragists to march along the entire length of the city's main thoroughfare, the Aceldama Way, shouting slogans and waving banners. On the day there were hundreds of marchers and hundreds more people lining the sides of the road, shouting support or abuse according to preference. Though with vigiles thick on the ground, none of the spectators dared throw anything. To add to that there were vigiles operating undercover... and the five special operatives were alert.

Dean and his assigned squad of vigiles had parted company with the ground crew and the other law enforcers early on, their task being to follow the march along the rooftops to the left according to the direction of travel. They had found the occasional crossbow-wielding malfeasor who had typically reacted with shock to their presence and rarely put up a fight. Only a few had the presence of mind to try to turn their weapons onto the law enforcement, and they were usually not in time to pull the trigger before they were overpowered. None of Dean's crew were seriously injured by the time the march was halfway done, though there had been the odd flesh wound.

However Dean's legs were burning and he was breathing heavily and raggedly by then, and he had been ruminating bitterly on how the kunoichi, who was managing the buildings on the opposite side of the way, must be a decade younger than him or more, and how the aedile had obviously stereotyped him as a typical burglar from his position of wealth and privilege. The fact that none of Noel, Ishtar or Aurelius were likely to have any of the requisite skill set and thus could only work on the ground did not factor into his internal monologue, or the fact that half his squad were breathing heavily and staggering too, yet made no complaint.

That monologue was abruptly broken however as, entering onto the next building top as the march and they progressed, they saw a figure lying at the side of the roof peering down into the thoroughfare and holding the expected heavy boltcaster. Hearing the booted tramp of the vigiles' approach the Satanist turned with a look of horror, trying in vain to manoeuvre the crossbow round to shoot at them. Dean got there first and send his buckler crashing into the cultist's face, breaking nose and teeth and sending him sprawling to hit his head hard against brick. His squad stepped forward to tie up the Satanist as they had done half a dozen times before this morning, marked for later collection.

'Ah, my sporting fellow, our second meeting.'

A voice had spoken from the shadows. From a pool of blackness cast by a tower stepped a tall figure wearing rich clothing. It was the Marquis of Aceldama. The vigiles started in consternation, but before they had any chance of reacting the Marquis waved a hand and the entire squad collapsed like puppets with the strings cut, limp as ragdolls. Dean stared at the pile of bodies in horror. He had no way of knowing if they were unconscious or dead.

His immediate instinct was to act tough.

'What are you doing here?'

'Merely getting a good view of the parade from up here. Lovely weather for it, don't you think?'

'While you pay no mind to this clown lying here with a crossbow? Don't make me laugh.'

The Marquis raised both hands and smiled sardonically. 'There are no flies on you, it seems.'

'What is your connection to these idiots?'

'None whatsoever, neither will you have any way of proving that there is one, even assuming someone in my position would be subject to investigation or prosecution in the first place.'

'There's always shooting first and asking questions later.'

The Marquis raised his eyebrows in mock surprise. 'Oh, and you think yourself and your little band would come off well in an encounter like that?'

Having seen the Marquis put the whammy on the vigiles squad Dean had no answer to this. It was quite tempting to tell the aristocrat to just fuck off, but this was no longer arguing from a position of strength – if he ever had been, which was doubtful.

'So this is a step up in the world for you, then?' said the Marquis, after an appreciable pause during which Dean had just glared.

'How do you mean?'

'Running law enforcement for the aedile.'

'He pays my hotel tab.'

'And that's the height of your ambition in life, then? What if someone was to offer you a better opportunity?'

'Why would they?' said Dean bitterly.

The Marquis raised his eyebrows again, this time with apparent sincerity. 'You limit your understanding and you limit yourself. You could do so much better.'

'And how is that?'

'I've said too much. For now.'

The Marquis backed away, retreating into the same inky pool of shadow from which he had come, a direction Dean could not look directly into without shading his eyes due to the glare of the morning sun. The aristocrat did not emerge again.

Dean frowned, wondering what had been said to him, but there was then a chorus of coughs and groans from the piled bodies of the aediles. A great flood of relief washed over the operative, blotting out any consideration of the speech's meaning. His team started getting to their feet, rubbing at bruises and contusions incurred by collapsing to the rooftop; it seemed they had only been unconscious, not dead.

'Urgh. What happened there?'

'The Marquis of Aceldama put the whammy on you all.'

'He was here?'

'Did you not see him? Any of you?'

There was a chorus of denials and shakings of heads. 'Great,' muttered Dean. 'Pull yourselves together, we have to get moving.'

9.

'The rally went ahead with only limited outbreaks of violence which were soon quashed by our forces. Only one crossbow bolt ended up being fired into the crowd, and we managed to contain the consequences of that. Conversely, in the rest of the city, there were nine fires and seventeen major crimes, none of which were contained or prevented by us.'

The aedile banged his fist on the table. 'Damn it, we have to get ahead of this! The Privy Council won't accept that this was a partial success on our part. They have difficulty believing in this Satanic conspiracy going on, even though I've said we've captured squealers. On the other hand the unchecked fires and criminality are very real. I'm hanging by a thread here. Throw me a bone!'

'There is the Marquis,' said Dean.

'So you say. And yet none of your team saw him. Why is that?'

'His spell must have blanked that section of their memories.'

'How convenient!'

'I know what I saw, he couldn't have been up there for any other reason than to orchestrate the violence.'

Lord Cromwell spread his hands. 'Look, I don't disbelieve you, particularly given the strange interest he seems to have taken in you. But there are a number of problems with this line. The first is wondering why the Marquis should associate himself with the losers and no-hopers who are in the Satanic conspiracy. He is already one of the richest men in the city, what has he to gain here? The second is that it is virtually impossible to challenge or accuse someone in his position unless he does something really egregious. I am but an earl, I can't just disappear him into some torture chamber the way I can with the bloody peasants.'

Dean scowled.

'And just what did that speech mean? Why has he focussed on you?'

'I have no idea,' the operative grated. 'I wish people would stop asking me.'

'It's not going to go away though.'

'I don't care!' hissed Dean.

'As you say,' the kunoichi interjected hastily, 'we have to come up with something that puts us ahead. We were really on the back foot.'

'Yes, let's get back on track. Any ideas anyone?'

There was an uncomfortable silence.

'Why can't we just confront the Marquis?' Dean said. The kunoichi winced.

Cromwell buried his hands in his hair and seemed on the verge of tearing it out. 'I told you! He is one of the most rich and powerful men in the city! A complaint from him to the royal family or the Privy Council would end my career and probably my life with it. We have no chance of doing anything to him unless he stabs one of the princesses in public and stands over her body holding the bloody knife waiting to be caught. And probably not even then.'

Dean shrugged. 'I suppose we'll just have to wait for the next massacre then.'

The aedile howled in fury. 'I can do without fucking smart comments like that at this time of night! Let's get one thing straight. If anything goes wrong in this city on my watch the Privy Council will have my blood. And I'm taking all of you with me. It is in all of your best interests to think of a solution. And you'd better do it. Dismissed.'

On the way out Noel made a general invitation to the team to join them for a drink in their hotel bar. Dean was impressed by the idea, thinking the general mood was exhausted, demoralised and dispirited and that it would improve relations within the team. In the event though only Aurelius accepted, who was of course the first person they had met in the city anyway; the kunoichi and the priestess of Astarte departed. Dean, Noel and Aurelius were left to sit at their hotel bar in an awkward anticlimactic silence, which stretched out for some time.

Eventually – and retaining sufficient prudence to wait till the barkeep was out of earshot – Dean spoke.

'Can't confront the Marquis,' he muttered, and took a long pull on his drink. 'My fucking arse.'

'You are too invested in this, my young friend,' said Noel. 'You need to disengage and calm down.'

Dean mumbled inaudibly.

'I might have thought of something,' said Aurelius.

Dean turned his eyes momentarily in the patrician's direction but made no comment.

'Go on?' prompted Noel.

'My family are patricians, one of the oldest houses in the city. We do not hold a title of nobility but we move in the same circles as the Marquis.'

'And?' said Dean.

'We could invite him to dinner.'

There was a long silence.

'That might *work*,' said Dean in tones of wonderment.

10.

The new plan required some considerable preparation.

To start with Dean and Noel both independently decided (and exhorted Aurelius at great length to comply) that Lord Cromwell should not know of this. This extended to the kunoichi and the priestess, whom, it was generally felt, had more loyalty to the aedile than any or all of the three men.

Meanwhile however, Dean and Noel still had access to an apparently bottomless expense account on the aedile's ticket, and they knew they had to dress for the occasion. Dean's great plaid looked like it had seen many years of rough living including being used for sleeping in night after night on mountain sides and under hedges, and that was because it had. So he had a new five yards of material made copying the old tartan exactly; when it was finished and worn, he looked like a dignified aristocrat himself. Even Dean had to do a double take, having never seen his oldest friend in that light. They had never had the money to dress like anything but tramps.

Dean himself decided to go one better than his previous disguise and wear the formal robes of a scholar. While far less exotic and impressive than the belted kilt, Dean looking at himself in the mirror did feel that he looked quite respectable. An approving nod from Noel made everything seem worth while, too.

Aurelius also did a double take on seeing Noel but made no comment; however, on seeing Dean, he stared with frank surprise. 'You wear that very well,' said the patrician. 'Were you a scholar once yourself?'

'Don't ask,' growled the operative.

Aurelius himself wore the toga that was his birthright as a patrician. Then came the next hurdle.

Dean and Noel had never met their young friend's family, and that was almost more daunting a prospect than dinner with the Marquis. Thus it was that they arranged to turn up some time earlier and make their introductions.

Aurelius turned out to be an only child, which surprised no one. His parents were typical upper class elders, grey haired and finely clad. Dean was the first to arrive and while they greeted him politely he could make out suspicion and unease behind their fixed expressions of mild welcome. These expressions changed completely as Noel entered. Clad in his new belted plaid the foreigner carried himself with a dignity and gravitas that made it seem that *he* was the highest ranking aristocrat in the room yet he was genuinely glad to be there. Aurelius's parents rushed Noel enthusiastically, uttering expressions of joyous welcome. Dean stared at them sidelong, feeling unwanted and left out. As the family backed away and servants – always with their eyes downcast and never speaking above a murmur – brought minute glasses of liqueur for everyone, Dean felt shabby and awkward next to his friend's quiet self assurance, even though his clothes were equally new. He had been dreading this dinner for many reasons, but now he knew that it would be as bad as he had thought or worse.

'So these are the new friends who got you the job with the aedile,' said Aurelius's mother, clearly as a conversation starter.

'Yes, that's exactly what happened,' interjected Aurelius hastily, staring at the two out-of-towners in panic.

'Can I express my greatest thanks that you have found my son a position,' said Aurelius's father, addressing his words mainly if not entirely to Noel. 'We had feared he might never settle to anything, other than his silly unarmed combat.'

Aurelius rolled his eyes, his fear apparently forgotten.

Conversation progressed in the same manner; it was obvious the parents felt more comfortable talking to Noel, and their speech was mostly in that direction. Such few sallies as were directed to Dean he responded to with brief, closed answers, and eventually the family gave up any pretence of trying to include him and conversed with Noel entirely, leaving Dean to stare at his glass or his nails. In Dean's excruciating discomfort this seemed to last a thousand hours at least, though it was probably only less than one.

And then – the Marquis.

The aristocrat swept into the room, and the centre of attention shifted permanently and irrevocably to that new centre. The Marquis carried himself as though he owned everything he surveyed, it only existed by his sufferance, and was in place only to owe allegiance to himself. He greeted the patrician family by name, clearly knowing them well, and then his eyes alighted on Dean and Noel. To his credit he showed virtually no discomfiture – Dean fancied the slight widening of the Marquis's eyes was visible only to himself.

'And who are these gentlemen?' said the aristocrat. 'Foreign relatives?'

'Ah no, these are our son's friends, my lord,'

'Ah my mistake. One never knows when long lost relatives are going to pop up from somewhere.'

Aurelius's parents uttered brief laughs at this feeble sally. Dean rolled his eyes – which the Marquis noticed. He raised his eyebrows but made no comment.

The mute servants, eyes downcast as before, led the party into the dining room with murmurs and gestures. Dean was relieved to see the family did not observe the counterproductive custom of reclining to eat, which gave people indigestion. The Marquis was seated at the head of the table, Aurelius's father opposite. To Dean's relief himself and Noel were seated by the elder patrician, with Aurelius's mother and himself on either side of the Marquis.

'So I understand your son is now working for Lord Cromwell?' said the Marquis and sipped at his Falernian.

'He is. We're very proud of him,' beamed Aurelius's mother.

'And these two foreign gentlemen are the ones who obtained young Aurelius the position?'

'Yes that's exactly what happened,' interjected Aurelius, entirely too quickly.

'Really,' said the Marquis in a manner that hinted he knew the true story anyway, and sipped at his Falernian again. The level had not diminished appreciably as though the aristocrat was only pretending to imbibe. Dean wished he had thought of this himself some time earlier. He was starting to feel somewhat intoxicated.

'So what exactly is it you do for Lord Cromwell?' the aristocrat asked.

Aurelius sputtered helplessly, muttering er and um, clearly thrown by the question. Dean was thinking of butting in with a pointed comment about investigating Satanic conspiracies and their possible sponsors when Noel saved the day. It was far from the first time this had happened.

'My dear Lord Aceldama, in my land work topics are considered very heavy for a pleasant dinner amongst friends. In our armed services, for instance, talking shop is forbidden at mess. Our young friend is probably also unused to being in the presence of one of your elevated dignity, lighter topics would put him at his ease.'

The Marquis appeared impressed, whether truly or feigned. 'You speak well, sir. I see by your garb that you are from the highlands of Caledonia.'

Noel himself now appeared impressed, and Dean was more inclined to bet that it was genuine. 'You recognise my tartan, sir, that *is* impressive.'

'I did much travelling in my younger days, trying to see all I could of the world, before I was forced to take on this title.'

Forced, thought Dean. That amount of money and power. Right.

'And yourself, my friend, you wear the robes of a scholar, where did you study?'

'The university of Praga,' said Dean without thinking and immediately cursed himself for a fool.

The Marquis raised his eyebrows. 'Now *that* is impressive. I can only salute your academic accomplishments.'

'We wished Aurelius would have gone to a prestigious university like that, but all he's ever applied himself to is his silly unarmed combat.'

'Mother!' hissed the junior patrician in mortified tones.

'I was in Praga on my Grand Tour, some forty years ago now,' said the Marquis and sipped his Falernian (which still had not decreased) while staring directly and heavily at Dean. Dean frowned and stared back, wondering what this meant.

'So what led you to leave Caledonia?' said Aurelius's father.

Noel smiled. 'My dear sir, in Caledonia a crust of bread, a piece of cheese and a morsel of mutton are considered a veritable feast. One does not experience the high life and good food such as this. I sought out other lands for my stomach more than anything.'

Dean had known Noel a long time and was pretty sure this wasn't the reason. Not that they had ever discussed it.

'And what led you to leave Praga, my high-flying scholar?' said the Marquis.

'I'm not from Praga, I'm from Byzantium,' said Dean and cursed himself inwardly again. He was feeling very drunk and seemed to be in a mental state where his mouth was talking for him and answering questions without any input from his brain – which was feeling very clouded. 'My studies came to an end so I went back. Never much liked the place.'

The Marquis seemed consternated at that, or at least Dean thought he could see that expression flash forth before he wiped it away and replaced it with bland smoothness. 'Byzantium! Once a great city, the greatest in the world, though sadly faded from past glories.'

'Yes, time and sorrow have descended upon it,' said Dean and drank heavily from his glass. Even to his own ears it seemed an odd statement and he could tell that his voice was starting to slur. He caught a look of concern pass between Aurelius's parents and felt a surge of irritation – which he realised was the belligerence of the drunk. Mercifully it seemed that an unspoken agreement went round the table to direct conversation away from him lest he disgrace himself. The next thing he found himself drinking was water, discreetly placed at his elbow by a servant. He hadn't been surprised, and was indeed somewhat relieved.

11.

Dean did not say anything else for the remainder of the dinner and spent much of it in a fog, part of this drunkenness but another part self-loathing and bitter reminiscences about the problems alcohol had caused him in the past – which were by no means small or few. Outside of this funk he was aware that most of the conversation was transpiring between Noel and the Marquis, though he was too woozy and self-recriminating to follow much of it, and was also aware that he was disgracefully eating more than was polite. Eventually the excruciation came to an end and Dean, Noel and the Marquis stood up to take their leave, Dean merely being able to smile or grimace or bow in leavetaking, unable to trust himself to speak, and the servants (possibly having been given preceding orders by Aurelius) directed the two parties to different exits. Dean found himself and Noel walking back through the streets of Potters Field, the alternating blasts of fresh air and the stink of the city doing something to finally clear his head.

'Well I guess I really fucked that up, huh?'

Dean would have taken any sincere criticism from Noel as the worst of bollockings from anyone else. He glanced at his companion guiltily and was surprised to see him smiling.

'Not at all, my young friend. You acquitted yourself admirably.'

Dean scowled. 'Don't take the piss I'm not in the fucking mood.'

'I am entirely sincere. If you wanted to deflect suspicion away from the idea that we're acting under orders from Lord Cromwell you couldn't have done it a better way.'

'Oh... okay,' said Dean, and smiled slightly, starting to feel more sober.

'Imagine a situation where one of our party stayed stone cold sober and asked loaded questions all afternoon – precisely as the Marquis himself did. That would have made it obvious that we have an agenda, and there would be no reason for two "foreign gentlemen" to be acting on their own accord so we would have to have been under orders from the aedile – who the Marquis already knows has Aurelius as an employee. For one of our party to be inebriated and make potentially damaging personal admissions merely proves that we are private individuals. Particularly when the more sober party is from Caledonia, where the best dinner you can expect is a horseshit sandwich.' Noel smiled. 'I even put a private word in with Aurelius's parents that you were acting the way Cromwell had told you to act, so you've not even put up a black there.'

'Wow... thank you. Sorry I did drop you in it though, I realise you were talking to the Marquis most of the time.'

'Oh I really have had worse dinners in Caledonia, whether or not we were eating horseshit. One thing is for sure though, the Marquis is fascinated by you. He kept asking about Byzantium and Praga and how I knew you. It was all I could do to keep deflecting his questions, I lost track of how many times I said I had been to neither of those places.'

Dean winced. 'What did you tell him in the end?'

'I got the impression that the Marquis would have been impossible to lie to, like all really smart people, and I did not make the mistake of trying. It was impossible to conceal that we were professional adventurers, but there was no reason to believe we were acting under orders from Cromwell. I managed to keep digressing into romantic retellings of our more legal exploits, more or less fictionalised, and Aurelius – bless him – fell for it hook line and sinker. He kept demanding more stories, even talked over the Marquis on one occasion which is putting up a major black even in Caledonia.

Though even his parents seemed entertained as well. I don't think Lord Aceldama learned anything valuable.'

'Great. Another partial success then. I actually feel better now.'

'Indeed! And, since I think we did more good than harm, I might even let you have another drink,' said Noel as they reached their hotel.

'Don't mind if I do!'

12.

Some days passed following the dinner and Dean and Noel heard nothing from either Lord Cromwell the aedile or the Marquis of Aceldama, though they met up with Aurelius occasionally. There was ample time for Dean to sober up from the dinner, have more drinking sessions, and subsequently consider, as he had before, his relationship with alcohol – though the only conclusion he had ever been able to draw was that it was a test of strength he would never win. Then – a summons from the aedile – very early in the morning. Dean was surprised to find himself, for once, not hungover.

'Have a look at this, see what you make of it,' said Lord Cromwell with obvious forced lightness and no preamble, tossing a scrap of paper onto his desk. The five operatives all stared at it.

The kunoichi was the first to pick it up. 'Latin not Greek. Someone literate but no scholar.'

Lord Cromwell ground his teeth in fury, his light veneer dropping away. 'I could do without smart comments like that at this time of the morning! If I wanted statements of the obvious I could do it my bloody self.'

The kunochi snapped her hand open theatrically and the paper fell back to the desk. It was an extreme reprimand for her statement and she was clearly offended. Though Dean realised, with a sinking in the pit of his stomach, that this must mean the content of the letter was very serious indeed. He snatched it up and read aloud.

'Greetings from the streets and sewers of Potters Field, where the gutters are filled with filth, faeces, spittle, semen, urine and blood. We write in the name of Satan, Lucifer, Mephistopheles and Leviathan, of Belphegor, Marbas, Ashtoreth and Asmoday. We are the allied cult of Satanists, the Unus Nusque, the Grey Order, the Brotherhood of Belphegor, those of no allegiance and of many, black magicians and hardened criminals. We are writing to inform you that our numbers have risen to the point where we outnumber the vigiles five to one. Surrender the city to us now, and there will be no need to massacre any more innocent people, which will be the result of a bloodbath we will orchestrate every week until our demands are met. Instead, if you let us have the town, we promise to buy all the vigiles and the aediles too a new pair of shoes each if we can get the money. Praise Hell Satan.' Dean dropped the letter to the desk, shocked to an extent he hadn't believed possible.

'Ashtoreth is a corruption of Astarte, demonised for propaganda purposes by the Christians. This is fake *and* offensive,' spat the priestess, flicking at the letter in genuine anger.

'The Unus Nusque and the Grey Order are two names for the same organisation,' said the kunoichi, speaking slowly and clearly still angry at being shouted at. 'And shouldn't that be Asmodeus?'

'I know people that have summoned that entity. It apparently refers to itself as Asmoday.' Dean said offhand. Everyone turned and stared at him. 'What?'

'Praise Hell Satan sounds fake,' ventured Aurelius, possibly for the sake of having an input and making a transparent attempt to be optimistic.

'I notice that there is no way of telling them that we actually accede to their demands,' put in Noel. 'I mean obviously they can't leave a return address, but still.'

'Ladies and gentlemen,' grated the aedile, his face livid, 'I thank you for your comments. They are all *very* smart and they are all quite useless. We are in the shit.'

There was a silence.

'But how did they know where to send the letter?' said Aurelius. Dean winced.

The aedile howled in rage. 'I am a public official, you unbelievably stupid shit! It was put in my office letterbox and I have no way of knowing who put it there!' Cromwell suddenly collapsed onto the desk, his head in his hands, possibly if not completely influenced by the fact that he had just insulted a patrician. 'I'm sorry,' he whispered. 'I've been under a lot of strain.'

The operatives exchanged glances over the aedile's bent back and, by unspoken agreement, moved a little way away to the back of the office. Ishtar grabbed the letter as she walked.

'Our sponsor's reaction is understandable,' said Noel in an undertone. 'We really are stuck what to do now.'

'There's a lot of evidence that it's fake but we can't rely on that,' said the kunoichi. 'And in a way it doesn't matter if there are fifty thousand Satanists or fifty. They can still kill innocent people and wreak havoc, there's just less or more of it. And every death is a tragedy for someone.'

'So what do we do then? Laughing boy clearly isn't up to giving us any more orders,' grated Dean, waving at Cromwell's desk. The aedile did not even move.

Ishtar shrugged.

'We pray.'

13.

Dean's immediate impulse was to laugh but looking at the priestess's serious face he knew better than to do so. The thought was at once followed by the memories of what he had seen Ishtar do – charm enemies to kill their friends, heal grievous injuries – and praying over a letter no longer seemed so strange.

'The siddhis arise at need, not at want. Astarte will know that innocent people are at threat and, if it is Her wish, grant the solution to this situation.' The priestess bowed her head and closed her eyes, holding the letter over her heart. The others looked down and closed their eyes also, though Dean glanced between them somewhat uneasily. He had the sudden incongruous thought as to whether he had ever prayed properly to the Magdalene.

Before long Ishtar snapped her head up. 'Right, we have a direction.'

'Huh?' said Aurelius brilliantly.

'A heading to lead us to the person who wrote the letter. Sir, do we have your permission to pursue this?'

The aedile did not look up, just waved his hand.

'OK, thanks. Let's go!'

14.

Outside it was high noon and the innocent citizens of Potters Field were going about their business which mostly involved eating or going to lunch, knowing nothing of the Satanic conspiracy in their midst or the evil beings who would destroy them for their twisted whims. The priestess strode purposefully through the streets followed by the rest of the team; Ishtar drew attention for the scantiness of her clothing but also respectful nods for her holy station.

As it turned out the destination was not even that far from the aedile's office. The team found themselves outside a downmarket hostelry called *The Golden Apples of the Hesperides.* They found a back alley adjoining the pub and subsequently located a small window where they could unobtrusively surveil the interior. Their target clearly had no idea how to evade pursuit and was blissfully unaware that he had attracted hostile attention. Their target was, in fact, not remotely impressive in the least.

'*This* twat wrote that letter?' whispered Dean.

'Shhhh!' hissed the priestess. The twat in question was an ill-favoured young man with unmanageable hair sticking up from a double crown, scrawny and ugly with wonky teeth, wearing the tunic of an unskilled labourer and noshing enthusiastically at a bowl of cheap stew with the manners of a pig.

'There has to be more to this, there has to,' muttered the kunoichi.

'That's as may be. Listen. Another of the blessings Astarte grants us in such situations is these paired stones. Take this one, and it will enable you to be party to our conversation.'

'What will you do?' asked Aurelius.

'Use my charm, of course. I don't need to be a priestess to do that!'
Tugging her top down even lower than it had been already, and
adding an extra wiggle to her hips, Ishtar sashayed down the alley
and into the bar.

As suggested, the remaining operatives listened to the stone, relaying
sound from inside the pub. The twat was, predictably, utterly
overawed that a girl of Ishtar's league was talking to him and even
deigning to notice him at all, and did not see anything suspicious
about this or even recognise (or consider significant if he did) the
fact that Ishtar was a priestess of Astarte. Perhaps his thought
processes were too simple to consider any of this. Dean concluded
that, had he been a betting man, this would have been the way he
would have set the odds. Surely no one of even average intelligence
could be that mesmerised by Ishtar's admittedly spectacular breasts
and thighs for that long or to that extent.

Meanwhile the priestess showed a different personality or facade
entirely, gushing, simpering and apparently on the intellectual level
of her target. Dean thought he had read or heard somewhere, or
possibly imagined for himself in a drunken haze one time, that
professional honey traps were generally plain or unnoticeable –
precisely like the kunoichi in fact – because anyone with half a brain
would realise that someone particularly beautiful would not just
randomly approach them without an ulterior motive in mind. Target
for today did not seem to have even half a brain, however.

In any case it was not long before Ishtar had persuaded the twat to
accompany her on a trip outside the bar, whatever job he might have
apparently forgotten, with the hinted promise of physical pleasures.
Thus did the fool follow the priestess into the alley, and thus did
Dean grab him round the neck and stick the point of one of his
holdout daggers into his skin.

'Talk or you're a dead man,' hissed the Byzantine.

15.

The idiot's bladder let go with a wet hiss and he gave a moan of despair. Dean snarled in disgust.

'I should kill you just for that, you fuckwitt!'

The priestess stepped in front of the target, closely flanked by the other operatives doing their best to look threatening, and her simpering demeanour sloughed away like a snakeskin. Even Dean was afraid.

'You wrote this!' she snarled, mashing the letter literally against the miscreant's face. 'You have blasphemed against the holy goddess Astarte and threatened the lives of innocent people. You deserve to die. Why did you do it!'

The twat started blubbing, tears and snot dribbling down his face. Dean's lip curled.

'The man told me to!'

'What man!'

'He was rich! He gave me a purse of gold. It's not my fault! I need the money!'

'What did he look like!' hissed Dean, shaking the fool so that his teeth rattled.

'Long hair. Eyepatch. Jewelled sword. Good clothes. Please, please don't kill me!'

'Gah!' shouted Dean, pulling the dagger away and shoving the idiot to the floor. 'Get away from me before you shit yourself as well.'

The miscreant huddled on the floor, shuddering and weeping with his head in his hands. A rising stench proved that he had, indeed, crapped in his tunic.

'The Marquis. It has to be,' said Ishtar.

'If we hand this guy over to Cromwell he can extract more information,' said Aurelius.

'No,' said the kunoichi quietly and hollowly, staring down at the floor, not making eye contact with anyone. 'We can't give this man to the aedile.'

Staring down at the pathetic figure on the floor, crouched in his own poo and wee, Dean felt a surge of guilt. He had a flash in his mind's eye of the broken, gibbering wreck that would be produced by the aedile's torturers, then summarily executed like all the rest. 'She's right. We can't.'

'I think in this case this man's main wrongdoing was being in the wrong place at the wrong time,' said Noel. 'Even if he is associated with the Satanists after all I do not think the punishment will fit the crime.'

'But why-'

'Aurelius, for once please be quiet,' said Dean wearily. He kicked out at the idiot's befouled arse. 'Go on. Get out of here. Thank your lucky stars and get yourself a clue.'

'I can go one better,' said Ishtar. She hauled the fool to his feet by the front of his tunic (since he was smaller than she was, this was not difficult) and forcefully planted a kiss on his forehead. The terrified expression smoothed over and he appeared to sleep. She lowered him gently to the floor of the alley. 'There. Now he will not remember us or the Marquis and will only think he drank too much and disgraced himself. I don't think it'll be a new experience for him.'

'So what do we do now,' said the kunoichi.

Ishtar set her jaw. 'Sub rosa,' she said.

16.

On hearing the words sub rosa the three natives of Potters Field immediately took on a new earnestness and made a beeline for the nearest street corner flower girl, buying a single rose from her and then seeking out a cheap hotel, the type usually frequented by prostitutes and their clients that rented rooms by the hour. The clerk raised his eyebrows at the motley crew who wished to book for sixty minutes. 'Good luck with your religious ritual, Priestess,' he said with an expression that said he meant *religious ritual* to mean *orgy*. Ishtar silenced him with a glare; he paled and went back to his gossip rag.

Inside the room the kunoichi clambered onto the bed and affixed the rose to the ceiling with an unidentifiable but still lethal looking metal implement. She got down and the three town natives stood in an arc, motioning the foreigners to stand completing a circle.

'This is the ritual of Sub Rosa,' said the kunoichi. 'It signifies that, beneath this rose, everything said must not be divulged to anyone else.'

Dean wondered why they hadn't just had the conversation in the alley rather than going through all the expense and rigmarole, and was forced to conclude the sub rosa ritual was kind of a big deal.

'As we have suspected,' said Ishtar, 'all indications point to the Marquis of Aceldama being behind the Satanic conspiracy. And yet our commander, the aedile Lord Cromwell, the Earl of Midian will not move against him despite clear and present danger to innocent lives.'

'Our fearless leader the aedile seems broken past the point of uselessness,' commented Dean, to frowns from Ishtar and the kunoichi.

There was a silence.

'I think you know what you have to do,' said Noel to break the tension. Dean, the kunoichi and the priestess nodded grimly.

'What's that?' said Aurelius. Dean groaned. The two women seemed not to realise the irony.

The priestess spoke without any hint of condescension. 'We take the law into our own hands.'

17.

The Marquis's house lay in a very large area of parkland on the extreme outskirts of the city, a place that had once been its own separate area from the town before the huge population growth stemming from various forms of progress. The operatives had applied every technique of stealth they could to themselves – from blacking their faces with grease mixed with soot on up – and set out, of course, to infiltrate Lord Aceldama's mansion in the dead of night, to find evidence of his wrongdoing or confront the man himself.

Creeping through the mixed grassland and woodland in the darkness bought back many, many unhappy memories for Dean, to the point he felt overwhelmed and on the point of breaking down. A few times the natives of Potters Field looked over with concern and asked if he was all right, to receive various forms of rebuttal; Noel, looking over sadly, had obviously already put two and two together and said nothing. Dean remembered a time when his life had been just going from one of these missions to another and living for nothing more to get blind drunk in between. A time from which he saw no hope of leaving and expected, even wished, to die before long as an end to it all.

A time from which Noel had saved him.

And yet this time was not that time. Now he was fighting to save innocent people and he appreciated the people on his team (whether or not they had divided loyalties or were hopelessly naive) and while he was indeed looking forward to consuming a very great deal of alcohol, he realised he hoped to drink with his new companions rather than alone and have the pleasure of their company rather than just seeking release in oblivion. And, with a breathtaking, paralysing shock, he realised he actually wanted to *succeed* in this mission. In the olden days he had only wanted to die.

He felt a weight lift within his heart, one that had been there so long he had long since ceased to notice it. For the first time for as long as he could remember he smiled. Noel, surreptitiously watching him without his younger friend noticing, smiled and relaxed as well.

But there was just one problem.

'This is too easy,' muttered the kunoichi for the hundredth time.

'Thinking the same thing,' whispered Dean, suddenly finding himself back in the present. There had been no walls, no guards, no groundskeepers, no wildlife other than herds of deer presumably kept for hunting. The Byzantine had expected wolves and bears and Magdalena knew what else to waste all his spell power on before he even got near the mansion.

'This doesn't bode well,' he said aloud.

'Quiet!' hissed Ishtar. But Dean thought he had a point.

They carried on through the parkland and eventually found themselves at the Marquis's mansion, which was huge and grand as was expected for a man in the lord's position. They skirted the house at a wide berth, varying their spacing, avoiding silhouetting themselves and all the other basic requirements of night work, but all the time having the paradoxically uneasy suspicion there was no need; none of them had the tell-tale sense of anyone watching. They eventually found what they considered to be a service entrance and chose a suitable route to it – the Marquis had not even bothered leaving clear space around his domicile and there were scattered hedges, clumps of trees, ha-has – not the strategy of a man wanting to conceal criminal wrongdoing. Or a man who cared about getting caught.

The operatives entered by the service door and found themselves in a scullery. To the team's consternation there was a girl in drab clothing slumped in a chair by the ashes of a fire; and she must have been a very light sleeper or supposed to be on duty or both, because she awoke with a start despite how quiet the operatives were being.

'Oh... hello,' she stammered. 'Can I help you?'

Dean was hoping they wouldn't have to kill this girl when Ishtar blew her a kiss. The servant smiled, let out a happy sigh and slumped back into her chair. Before long she was snoring.

'May Astarte go with you,' the priestess muttered and looked around, finding another door and striding towards it purposefully, less concerned now with being quiet.

The team made their way through several more rooms. They encountered a few more servants who were either napping or going about their business, and those who awakened or were already awake were soon sent into a happy dream by Ishtar like the first girl.

'We should have brought priestesses on our previous missions,' whispered Noel to Dean.

'Yes,' muttered Dean, staring at Ishtar's barely-clad legs and ass.

Eventually the operatives found a room that was clearly the Marquis's study and the kunoichi immediately made a beeline for a large writing bureau. She pulled out some lockpicks and rapidly had it open, revealing an enormous number of compartments and more loose documents scattered in front. Dean and the kunoichi started grabbing them at random, eyes going wider and wider with each one.

'This is crazy,' whispered the kunoichi. 'Records of invoices for stockpiles of weapons. Correspondence with known underworld figures. Letters from the Satanist organisations signed off with Blessings in the name of Belphegor and the like, for fuck's sake. This is incriminating as hell. Why is this house not defended at all? Why is all this stuff barely guarded?'

'Because, my dear, it is protected by *me*.'

The five law enforcers wheeled as one, Dean and the kunoichi scattering papers and scrolls to the floor. In the doorway of the study stood the Marquis.

He extended a finger and pointed at the priestess's heart.

'Die,' he said.

Ishtar's eyes rolled up and she collapsed to the floor like lead.

'NO!' screamed Aurelius.

18.

'I'll deal with you later,' said the Marquis and raised his other hand in Dean's direction. From the palm sprang a gobbet of matter which flew into the Byzantine's chest with enough force to knock him backwards into the wall. There it exploded in a mass of sticky strands which stuck Dean fast and covered him like a cocoon, leaving his head free. Otherwise, he was unable to move.

'NOOOOOO!' screamed Aurelius again, tears pouring from his eyes.

'Aurelius, don't!' cried various of the operatives, but the patrician had gone mad with grief and rage. Forgetting all notion of tactics and teamwork, he rushed straight at the Marquis.

'Ah, the old family's boy who fancies himself an aikidoka. Onegeishimas!' The Marquis bowed rigidly from the waist, straightening just as Aurelius's insane rush reached him. He sidestepped casually and seemed to grab at the patrician slightly. Aurelius was sent careering off balance into a corner, barely able to halt himself and keep his footing. Dean could see the shock on his face, but it hadn't contained his mad grief. He rushed the Marquis again, who seemed barely to dodge and just to poke Aurelius slightly, but the patrician was sent careering into a wall with vicious force. Dean groaned.

Aurelius pushed himself off the wall, wincing; he had hit his head. But he looked up at the Marquis, tears still running down his face, and made a more cautious approach, hands in a more considered stance. The Marquis gave a look that was bored and annoyed, reached out to Aurelius's leading hand... and the patrician was sent swinging vertically like a pendulum over the Marquis's head to slam into the floor with horrible velocity. Dean winced at the sound of multiple bones crunching. The patrician did not rise again.

'Who's next?' said the Marquis conversationally.

The kunoichi reached into her clothing and produced a handful of sharp metal implements which she hurled at the Marquis, the whole operation almost too fast to see. The Marquis raised his eyebrows; the missiles stopped abruptly and fell out of the air. Dean saw to his horror that the kunoichi also was crying silently. She produced another handful of missiles which she threw with the same result. She tried a third and fourth time with alternate hands and blinding speed, a tactic perhaps designed to drain an opponent's energy. They kept stopping as though hitting an invisible wall.

'So it is to be throwing weapons, then?' said the Marquis. He reached into his cape and produced a long infantry dart, the kind thrown by legions en masse from behind their shield walls, almost a foot of pointed and sharpened iron with flights for accuracy. He reached back over his shoulder and hurled it overhand... and the kunoichi screamed and collapsed as the dart went completely through her leg with the awful loud crack of her femur being snapped in two.

Even with her thigh bent horribly beneath her and blood slowly forming a pool around her stricken body the kunoichi still found the will to fight. She started hurling her tessen with killing force, with the Marquis frowning as he telekinetically diverted them to crunch into the wall, sending shards of plaster raining down. But before long:

'Enough of this,' said Lord Aceldama and removed his eyepatch. It somehow surprised no one to see there was a perfectly normal and functioning human eye beneath which matched his other one. He made a horrible squinting expression... and a ravening blast of smoking ruby light blazed from the revealed orb to burn a hole through the kunoichi's stomach and into the floor beneath. She collapsed forward, finally out of the battle.

Now there was only one operative left.

'Ah, the Caledonian fighter,' said the Marquis. 'Shall we try our skills?'

'That we most certainly will,' said Noel, throwing his belted plaid's cloak behind him and drawing his basket-hilted broadsword and his sgian dubh dagger in his characteristic southpaw array. The Marquis too drew his own jewelled weapons, with the rapier in his left hand and his dagger in his right.

Dean hadn't felt he could get any lower, but still his heart sank. Seeing this he had a terrible feeling as to how the fight would go.

The two men gave battle. Dean had known Noel many years and from the start it was clear he was outmatched. Sweat broke out on the Caledonian's forehead, and continued to pour down his face, while the Marquis duelled almost casually as if he were at a garden party, even though Noel was larger and his weapons were much heavier. Before long Lord Aceldama was making little cuts and stabs on Noel like duelling scars worn by university students, clearly toying with the Caledonian, while Noel could not even get near the Marquis. When Noel's breathing grew ragged it was the kiss of death.

The Caledonian tried his final trick as he had to, even though Dean had an awful fear as to what would result. 'You fight well, my aristocratic friend,' gasped Noel, barely able to get the breath to speak the words. 'But I have had to battle for my life on a daily basis since before I achieved manhood. And-' he threw his weapons into the air, catching them again in the opposite hands, 'I am not left handed.'

'You fight well yourself, northerner,' said Lord Aceldama. 'But I have had cause to fight more than you may think. And,' he repeated the trick exactly the same, now with a right-handed rapier and main gauche dagger, 'I am no southpaw either!'

Noel's jaw sagged open in shock, and Dean knew that the fight was lost.

The Marquis rushed the Caledonian, with his face contorted into cold fury, and it rapidly became clear just how much the lord had been holding back; Noel was now hopelessly outmatched. When Aceldama finally sent his steel through his opponent's torso it was as much to put everyone out of their misery as anything. Noel, exhausted and with his morale broken, stared down at the rapier as the Marquis withdrew it and fell forward into a crumpled heap.

'NO!' screamed Dean, unable to refrain from starting to weep uncontrollably himself.

'And now it is just you, Byzantine.'

The Marquis gestured and the sticky mess holding Dean to the wall evaporated as though it had never been. 'Your friends are all dead. Why don't you have a crack? Your magic first, I think.'

Dean knew his position was hopeless and he was being toyed with like a mouse, but he had to try, and he still burned with anger and grief.

The Byzantine gestured and his magical darts of force lanced out, predictably to evaporate in front of the Marquis. Even more predictable was that the aristocrat was not even remotely affected by Dean's basic sleep spell, and appeared insulted that he had even tried it. As Dean unleashed his final and most powerful spell, a ravening stream of flame, Aceldama merely stood still and let the fire pour round him like a stream around a rock. Dean could only stare at him in hatred.

'A futile attempt. You should be a more powerful spellcaster at your age. Let's see your martial skills.'

Dean knew this would be even more pointless than the magic. Any fighter that could beat Noel could defeat himself with less than a third of the effort. It would have been more dignified to just throw his arms down and refuse. But his rage and grief were such that he drew out his rapier and buckler and rushed the Marquis anyway.

This went about as well as could be expected. The Marquis parried Dean's attacks with minimal effort, looking disdainful and annoyed, eventually to frown and disarm the Byzantine of his sword with a slight flick of his wrist, leaving Dean with his right hand empty and his fingers stinging. Pursing his lips with irritation, Aceldama gestured and the buckler flew out of his opponent's left hand into the wall, leaving Dean apparently unarmed. The Marquis brought his own rapier in front of him and placed the point against Dean's stomach.

'A bit poor, to be honest. Your swordsmanship should be better by this point in your life also. We will have ample time to work on that in the future.'

'How is that!' Dean snarled, ignoring the sword point at his stomach and keeping his eyes locked on the Marquis's.

'When you come and live with me in this mansion, of course.'

'And why would I do that!'

'Because, Dean, I am your father.'

'I know who my father is.'

Both men kept their gaze locked on each other, Dean's blazing with hatred and anger, but there was a shift of awareness in both minds to the crumpled figure in the great plaid lying stricken and bleeding not far away. The Marquis's eyes widened in fury. 'Fool! You would be inheriting into the purple!'

'I don't care! Why are you with the Satanists?'

'My dear boy, I am not *with* them. They are deluded fools. The vast majority are pathetic no-hopers who only joined up because they can't get a girlfriend. Even the black magicians are hopelessly limited. They are merely a tool I finance so long as I can use them to sabotage Democracy Now.'

'Why are you doing this? Innocent people are dying!'

'They are only peasants! My dear boy, do you not even know what a Marquis is?'

'Yes I know that! It's the highest rank of the aristocracy that can be reached without being a member of the royal family.'

'And what good do you think universal suffrage and democracy would achieve for a man in my position, with all my lands and wealth?'

'Er... not very much?'

'Of course not!' The Marquis paused. 'Though arguably, I do what I do out of boredom.'

'You utter *cunt!*'

The Marquis clicked his tongue. 'Foul language, foul language. It is depressing that a man your age should comport himself in such a manner. You will have to be taken well in hand.'

'I'll never have anything to do with you. I will die first. And the only reason you have so much better skills than all the rest of us is because you had unlimited time and money to train and hire tutors. Some of us fight and live just to survive.'

'So you say. And perhaps it is true. Still, only your body needs to be in my mansion, at least initially. The rest I can handle with *mind control*. After a few months perhaps you will come around.'

Dean felt a will of enormous power clamp down upon him and hold him rigid like a fly in amber. He was locked in place even more effectively than when the Marquis's spell had stuck him to the wall. Waves of force beat down upon his mind like a raging waterfall. He knew that the power was too great, and he would succumb.

And yet, he thought of his friends – and with a shock, realised that he had come to see them as this.

He thought of the innocent civilians of Potters Field, preyed on by the rich and blighted by corruption and now randomly murdered to satisfy this evil aristocrat's selfish whims. He thought of the aedile, bellowing impotently from behind his desk, finally faced with a threat to the city he couldn't handle.

And finally he thought of the crumpled figure in the belted plaid. And that gave him the strength he needed.

With his last reserve of will Dean thrust his body forward. He walked forward onto the rapier, allowing it to pierce him through and through, and meanwhile reaching into his clothing and pulling one of the multiple holdout weapons he always carried.

The Marquis's eyes widened with shock. 'No! What are you doing!'

'I die, you die, don't ask why. *Dad.*'

Dean stabbed his concealed dagger up under the Marquis's xiphoid process and hopefully into his heart. The eyes, still wide with shock, grew glassy and rolled up. The Marquis toppled backwards, hand still locked on the rapier with which Dean was impaled, taking the Byzantine down with him. Son fell bodily on top of father, each driving steel into the other.

'I win,' hissed Dean into the lord's ear. There was no response.

19.

A silence fell for an indeterminate time.

Dean knew that he was dying. The pain he was in was breathtaking, and let him know that his alimentary canal had been pierced. Without magical healing that was an automatic death sentence and their healer had been the first to be taken out. Still, at least he had saved the city, probably. And with the Caledonian dead he realised he no longer wanted to go on living himself.

The silence lasted a while longer and Dean thought he had lost consciousness at some point when he heard a weak cough. A cough he would have recognised anywhere.

'*Noel!*'

'It is I,' came a bare whisper, with a weak laugh. 'Listen. I don't know how much longer I have to live. But I have an idea. Remember when we were in Hibernia?'

'Yes... Yes, I do.'

'Ishtar... you have to bring her back.'

'Yes... I will.'

Dean was still impaled on the Marquis's rapier, his own dagger driven deep under the lord's ribs. The first thing was to drag himself off the steel. Dean pushed his arms down and started pressing. The pain increased to the point that his vision and thinking ceased to function, but he knew beneath it all that he had to succeed... and he would certainly die rather than give the man in the great plaid cause for disappointment.

Dean finally pulled himself up and off the Marquis's steel (fortunately it was slender and bent quite a bit) and collapsed sideways, gasping, the newly opened wounds in his front and back seeping blood and his internal injuries no doubt doing the same or worse. But he knew what he had to do.

He crawled over to Ishtar's body and rolled her onto her back. He knelt above her and joined the heels of his hands together, making sure to keep his arms locked straight. He located his hands at the midst of her sternum and started thrusting the middle of her ribcage down several inches at a time with brutal force.

Some believed the lungs should be inflated every so often with the rescuer's own breath. Others believed this was of little effect.

Dean lost all track of time but he kept compressing Ishtar's heart until such time as her eyes opened, she screamed in agony, turned to the side and vomited. Dean collapsed on his back, his endurance finally gone.

'I think you broke my ribs,' the priestess croaked in pain.

'Yes, that does happen.'

'Astarte, aid me.' Strength flooded into Ishtar and she stood up, looking almost normal save for vomit down the front of her cleavage and naked stomach. With the healer standing and back in the game it was not long before the rest of the operatives could be brought back, largely intact except for bloodstains and shock.

All of them stared down at the Marquis, lying with his eyes rolled up and a holdout dagger shoved diagonally up under his ribs.

'Heal him,' said the kunoichi. 'And gather up all this evidence. He must stand trial,'

'Roger, roger,' said Ishtar, not without some irony.

It was only as they were leaving that Dean had a terrible feeling. He grabbed hold of Noel's tartan and pulled him back.

'How much did you hear?' he whispered in horror.

Dean put a hand on his younger friend's shoulder.

'I won't tell anyone,' he said.

20.

That might have been the end of that particular revelation and nothing might have come of it. But unfortunately for Dean and Noel the kunoichi happened to have been partially conscious as well, and she, of course, had always owed primary loyalty to Cromwell. Also, of course, the operatives had taken the law into their own hands, carried out a home invasion of one of the richest and most powerful men in the city, visited upon him scenes of incredible violence and robbed large quantities of his most personal documentation.

Thus it was that the five operatives found themselves once again in front of the aedile's desk. Except this time, there were no chairs, no wine, and heavily armed Praetorians guarding every exit. And this time Lord Cromwell was *really* mad.

Front and centre of the operatives was Dean. All of the team had cleaned up after their final battle but Dean in particular was wearing his new scholar's robes, the first time he had worn them in this office. The Byzantine stood rigid, looking defensive – and angry.

The aedile stared at him with incandescent fury.

'I'll deal with you first,' hissed Cromwell. 'So. Son of the Marquis.

'When I first saw you you were dirty, your face was filthy, you were down and out, dressed in rags and engaged in scamming the public out of money. When you were working missions for me you were a bit cleaner but still dressed like a tramp. I never before saw you in those crackerjack clothes. I would not have connected you with the richest man in this city in a thousand years.

'But now that I see you there, dressed up like King Shit of Turd Mountain with an expression like you're waiting for the cat to come in for a piss, I don't know how I or any of us could ever have been so stupid. You are the *spit* of the Marquis. You look virtually identical.

He must have realised you were his son straight off. I can't believe none of us did. It's hard to believe you didn't know in advance, or guess.

'Let's set a few things out early doors. You have none of the protections afforded to a Potters Field citizen. I could have you *crucified.* Or hung, drawn and quartered. Or disfigured, dismembered and chained up to starve. If you knew you were the Marquis's son and didn't tell us you have endangered your compatriots and critically endangered me. I have more to lose than you could possibly realise. And I am not a forgiving man. You had better explain yourself... quickly. TALK!'

Dean stared back at the aedile in anger and defiance, then dropped his gaze and sighed, his shoulders sagging.

'I grew up in Byzantium with what I believed to be my mother, my father and my older sister. There was never any love lost between my supposed parents and I, they bankrolled my education but I always felt I was an unwanted imposition on their lives. I never resembled my father at all, my mother only slightly, though I did look like what I thought was my sister. She was a strange girl, largely housebound, often weeping, few suitors. I always felt I could engage with her if I tried but she would keep bursting into tears before long and after a while I guessed the servants had been detailed to keep us apart. I went away to college as soon as I was able, met a girl in university but it didn't work out. However, by then, from incidental bits of evidence I'd been able to gather over the years I had concluded that what I had thought was my sister was actually my mother. She had been impregnated out of wedlock and my grandparents had created this deception to avoid scandal. Knowing all this contributed to my permanent estrangement from my family in my mid twenties. I can never go home again.'

Dean stared into the aedile's eyes, both of them burning with anger. 'And yes, I have no doubt now that my father was the Marquis. I never found any letters or anything but it all fits. And all these are memories which I have done my best to bury and blot out with alcohol. I would never have resurrected them or told them to any of you had you not threatened me with crucifixion. That's some great leadership skills right there! *Aedile*.'

'But how do you have a name like Dean when you're from Byzantium?' said Aurelius, brilliant as usual.

Dean ground his teeth in fury. 'Fool! I haven't used my real name in decades!'

'I don't use my real name either,' said Noel in an attempt to lighten the atmosphere. It didn't work.

Dean and Cromwell glared at each other for a few moments longer before the aedile, surprisingly, dropped his eyes. 'I am sorry to hear that. You have clearly had a difficult time of it. I apologise for making you bring it up. I hope you understand it was necessary.'

Dean made an irritated noise with his mouth but was clearly thrown.

'Now then, the rest of you. You have carried out an illegal house entry, arrest without a warrant, vastly excessive use of force against a citizen and unlawful seizure of documentation. All of this would be more than enough to see you all executed... had the evidence against the Marquis not been so comprehensively damning!'

The aedile, incredibly, cracked a smile for absolutely the first time ever, reached beneath his desk and produced a tray with a bottle of Falernian and six glasses. The jaws of the operatives sagged open as one. 'Well done everyone! Damned good show.'

Cromwell turned to the Preatorians. 'I don't think we'll be needing you any more. Please bring some chairs in on your way out.'

There was much muttering and grumbling amongst the elite guards who clearly considered the task beneath them, but before long the operatives were seated in front of the aedile's desk sipping wine in a notably more relaxed atmosphere.

'Now then,' said Cromwell. 'There is good news and bad news. The Marquis of Aceldama has been given time to depart.'

As one the natives of Potters Field lowered their gazes and shook their heads. Dean and Noel just looked confused.

'What is that?' said the Byzantine.

The aedile sighed. 'In this city there is a major cultural taboo against imprisoning anyone. Non citizens can be subjected to some truly awful punishments (sorry about the context in which I brought those up) whereas citizens are always entitled to a quick beheading with a very sharp sword. However, when the malfeasor is rich and powerful this isn't an option, not really. And so... time to depart.'

'Exile,' supplied the kunoichi. 'The guilty party must put their affairs in order and go far from the city, never to return. In theory this means they can no longer influence events in Potters Field or gain illegal income from criminal activities there-in but a lot of the gang bosses and hereditary kingpins still manage this.'

'However, it will limit the Marquis's hold on the Satanists, and they are a generally pathetic force who can be easily contained by our standard uniformed services,' said Cromwell. 'So, while I may still have need of you all, it is unlikely the situation will ever again become so desperate.'

'I'm an old man,' said Noel with a smile. 'I deserve a quiet retirement rather than fighting criminals and crawling through sewers.'

'I'll bear that in mind,' said the aedile offhand, not getting the joke.

'So what's the bad news?' said Aurelius.

Dean planted his face into his palm.

'How about we all go for a celebratory drink,' said Noel hastily.

Cromwell waved a hand. 'You all carry on. I still have a mountain of paperwork to clear up.'

Much to Dean's surprise, this time, the kunoichi and the priestess agreed to accompany the others for the first time ever. To supply themselves with an ironic sense of closure nothing seemed better to the operatives than to visit *The Golden Apples of the Hesperides*, where they drew a lot of stares from the rest of the clientele still dressed in their dusty labouring gear and their friend from before was absent, possibly gone to launder his tunic. There was no Falernian, but rough resined wine was actually a novelty.

'Gonna seduce any more guys today, sis?' said the kunoichi with a smile, elbowing Ishtar in the ribs, and lowering her hood, possibly the first time Dean had seen her do this.

'Get lost!' laughed the priestess, giving the kunoichi a playful shove and swigging her wine.

Dean did a double take. 'You're *sisters?*'

'Twins, actually.'

The Byzantine looked between them. Other than the kunoichi having long hair she and Ishtar had essentially the same face, even the same lopsided grin. Dean realised that he had only ever seen the spy in various disguises and headgear, or fully robed or hooded, but having seen her fight she clearly had the same physique as the priestess as well. But of course a deep cover operative would dress to avoid attention and a priestess of a love goddess would be clothed to attract it.

'You think because we look and act different we can't be related? You have much to learn about women.'

'You walked right into that, my young friend,' said Noel, winking.

'Fuck off, dad,' said the Byzantine and took a long draught of wine.

The others raised their eyebrows.

'You both look very nice,' said Aurelius with puppy-dog earnestness.

'Thank you! It takes a born patrician to know how to talk properly to girls.'

'Fuck that and fuck you all. Lest we forget I'm the only one who actually managed to stab the fucking villain.'

The others all howled in derision and started throwing peanuts at him.

After several more drinks there came the time of leaving. The younger operatives went their separate ways while Dean paused outside the bar, still in his scholar's robes, and Noel waited for him. Despite a considerable quantity of wine the Byzantine seemed reasonably sober.

'Going anywhere nice?' said the Caledonian.

'Do you know,' said the Byzantine, 'I might go and have a look at the university.'

'Have a good time,' said Noel, waving.

The Caledonian walked away, heading for a tavern where he had a romantic assignation with the proprietress. But as he left he turned and looked back at the other man. He was striding off in his scholar's robes with a new straightness to his back and purpose to his movement.

Noel smiled.

'My boy, you have come far,' he said.

COMING SOON... "MAGDALENA"

Printed in Great Britain
by Amazon